~ ARISE ~

SKYE MALONE

Arise
Book Four of the Awakened Fate series

Copyright © 2015 by Skye Malone

Published by Wildflower Isle | 1567 Highlands Drive NE, Suite 110-404
Issaquah, WA 98029
www.wildflowerisle.com

ISBN: 978-1-940617-17-6
1-940617-17-0

Library of Congress Control Number: 2014906856

Cover design by Karri Klawiter
www.artbykarri.com

PRONUNCIATION GUIDE

Aveluria (av-eh-LUR-ee-uh)

Dehaian (deh-HYE-an)

Driecara (dree-eh-CAR-uh)

Greliaran (greh-lee-AR-an)

Ina (EE-na)

Inasaria (ee-na-SAH-ree-uh)

Jirral (jur-AHL)

Lycera (ly-SER-uh)

Neiphiandine (ney-fee-AN-deen)

Niall (nee-AHL)

Nialloran (nee-ah-LOR-en)

Nyciena (ny-SEE-en-uh)

Ociras (oh-SHE-rahs)

Prijoran (prih-JOR-an)

Renekialen (ren-eh-kee-AHL-en)

Ryaira (ry-AIR-uh)

Sieranchine (see-EHR-an-cheen)

Siracha (seer-AH-cha)

Sylphaen (sil-FAY-en)

Teariad (tee-AR-ee-ad)

Torvias (TOR-vee-ahs)

Velior (VEH-lee-or)

Yvaria (ih-VAR-ee-uh)

Zekerian (zeh-KEHR-ee-en)

PROLOGUE

WYATT

I hated bullets. They got in the way of everything.

Blood dripping down my arm, I slowed to a walk while I watched the car race off. That scale-skin girl was in the back of it, and my cousin too, the latter of whom was responsible for the shotgun damage to my shoulder.

The bastard.

A growl slipped from me. I didn't bother to hold it back. I was in a field; it wasn't like there was anyone to hear me. But I'd been so close. So *damn* close and if Noah and his stepsister hadn't shown up with a car and a shotgun just as I was about to *finally* get my hands on that thing…

The growl grew stronger. Noah disgusted me. The betrayal of our calling, our *mission*, wasn't even the half of it. He'd gone so far as to get *involved* with one of them. And sure, the fish girl was hot; her kind were that way on purpose. But how anyone could let themselves actually *fall* for a creature like that was beyond me. Just the feel of her skin, or her legs around yours, with the knowledge either one could change into scales or that *tail* thing… repulsive didn't come close.

And that wasn't even bringing into it their manipulative bullshit, and how they could take away your will with a touch.

Anyone who stayed near something like her obviously enjoyed being a victim.

And so they deserved what they got.

I glanced to my shoulder while the car vanished over a small rise in the farmland. Light like the glow of lava showed beneath the tear in my shirt, obscuring the wound and steadily closing it up. My changed skin had absorbed most of the damage from the shot Noah had taken at me, although with a gun that size, some of the shell's impact had still gotten through. It wasn't bad, though. Distance had helped. If I'd been closer to the car when he pulled the trigger and he'd had better aim, it might've been a different story.

One more thing the pretty-boy bastard had to pay for.

I turned back toward the silos, letting my skin become more human while I went. The structures showed in sharp relief against the clear blue sky, and the midmorning sun revealed my younger brothers still trying to catch their breath by the nearest tower's side. Owen had his hand braced on the metal wall, while Clay was bent double. Even over the distance, I could see they looked like they wanted to puke.

Grimacing, I walked back toward them. I hoped the fish girl was heading for the ocean so we could track her there. I was sick of farmland.

Clay looked up. "You let her escape?"

"Shut up."

Still breathing hard, he resorted to a glare in response.

I ignored it, moving past him. Clay hadn't been able to take me in a fight in his life and he knew it. Words were the worst he could do to me. And the fact wasn't lost on Owen either. Two years older than Clay and a year younger than me, he wouldn't risk challenging the status quo for that guy's sake. Not if it ended him up answering to Clay.

And besides, they hadn't been able to catch her either.

Damn fish.

I rounded the side of the silo and started back toward the warehouse at the far end of the grain company property. Up ahead, police cars bounded down the country highway and then whipped tight turns into the warehouse parking lot. I sighed. Cops were nearly as bad as bullets, and for basically the same reason. Dad's guy, the puny Doctor Harman Brooks, would clear them out fast, though. He wouldn't want anyone poking around his precious laboratory. And as for that couple standing by their green sedan beside the warehouse, their heads turning as if they were searching for someone… whatever. They were probably friends of Harman's too.

Dad marched from the warehouse. Brock wasn't with him. My lip twitched toward a snarl. If that little bastard had taken the opportunity to kill the fish we had tied up in Harman's lab while I was busy chasing down the girl, I'd damn well make him pay.

After all, I wanted to kill a scum-sucker more than I'd ever wanted *anything*.

Stories said it felt wonderful, taking a dehaian's life with your bare hands. Their magic running into you while their blood poured out, filling you with a high more powerful than any drug could provide – all of which just got stronger the more scale-skins you killed. Earl hadn't been able to tell us much about it. After a fish bastard put their magic on his daughter – turning Jeri into his little slave up till the day she killed herself to make the longing stop – Earl had gone blind with rage. He'd taken the guy out so fast, the fish probably hadn't known what hit him, and Earl had been too distracted by what the guy did to Jeri to really enjoy the killing.

But I needed to feel what it was like. I needed the craving inside me to end, to finally be satisfied. It gnawed at me like a hunger, just like I knew it did for anyone who wasn't as pathetic as Noah, his brother, or their dad. But until those dehaians who'd just escaped us, the fish Earl killed had been the first one we'd heard of in my lifetime. They were hard to find, the scale-skins. They looked like humans, mostly acted like humans, and there wasn't much to set them apart from the herd besides a weird sense of *wrongness*, like they weren't the same as other people and didn't quite fit in. But that was difficult to detect, especially since I was starting to suspect they intentionally surrounded themselves with humans to disguise that sense.

I'd give anything to get my hands on a dehaian and kill them slow, savoring every bit of how amazing it would feel.

None of that would happen if the cops reached them first.

Dad strode toward me. "She got *away*?" he snarled, his voice low while his gaze took in me, Clay, Owen, and the complete lack of fish girl between us all.

"Noah was there," I explained.

Disgust flashed over Dad's face, at least until he spotted the blood on my arm and anger supplanted the expression. Grabbing my shoulder, he muscled me back from the cops.

I let him push me. He was bigger and stronger for now.

"Idiot," he snapped, throwing a glance to the police. "What're you doing, letting them see you–"

"Sir?" came a guy's voice.

Dad turned as one of the cops walked toward us. An annoyed sound escaped him and his grip tightened on my shoulder. "Say you ran into something," he ordered in a low mutter.

I didn't respond. The fish and Noah were getting farther away with every second. We should leave, and if the police tried to interfere, we ought to just handle them.

Though I supposed 'handling them' would be difficult for even Harman to cover up.

"Did you see what happened here, sir?" the cop asked.

Dad glanced to Harman. The doctor caught sight of the guy coming our way and immediately rushed over.

"Officer," Harman called. "Officer, this is a… he works with me. They, um… it was his son…"

The cop's face shut down as he looked between us and the old man. My brow furrowed. Dad's son?

I scanned the parking lot, suddenly realizing I still hadn't seen Brock. I couldn't feel him anywhere either. He hadn't stopped hiding, and by now, he really should have.

"What–" I started.

"I need to talk to my boys." Dad muscled me back again and looked to Harman. "And you."

The doctor swallowed hard. "I-if you'll just excuse us," he said to the officer. Harman turned to one of his assistants, a toothpick of a guy barely out of his teens, wearing a lab coat several sizes too large. I recognized him. He'd been one of the cops we'd scoped out back in that hick town, Reidsburg, where the fish girl lived.

"Aaron," Harman said, "could you finish explaining to the police what they need to be doing here?"

The assistant shifted his weight and gave a shrug that I assumed was meant to stand in for actual agreement.

Harman skirted wide of us while he hurried away from the officer. Dad followed him back around the corner and behind the cover of the warehouse.

"What–" I tried again.

Dad made a silencing noise and then motioned sharply for Owen and Clay to get farther out of sight.

"Make a sound at what I'm about to say and I'll knock your teeth out," Dad snapped to us all in a low voice.

I shivered, wanting to do that to him if he didn't get on with it soon.

He didn't seem to notice my tension. His jaw muscles jumped

and his lip curled as though barely holding back a snarl. With a dark glance to Harman, he seemed to struggle to speak the words. "Brock's dead."

My shivering grew stronger. Colors became heightened, as did sounds, and heat rushed through my skin as it changed.

Dad shoved me against the wall. "Stop it."

He tossed a glance to Owen and Clay, including them in the order.

"What happened?" I managed, the words only marginally coherent through my growl.

"The scum-sucker boy took a shotgun to him. Close range."

A breath left me. Goddamn it, I'd *had* that fish. He'd been right in front of me, all chained up and helpless, and if Dad hadn't kept me from killing him when we'd had the chance…

My gaze found Dad, every twitch of his muscles and drop of sweat on his face visible to my sharpened vision. He'd stopped us when we'd tried to use Noah's stepsister as bait in California, and the fish had gotten away as a result. He'd stopped us from breaking into the stepsister's house in Kansas and forcing her to tell us where the scale-skin lived, and only Harman's phone call had put us on the girl's trail again. Every time we had the chance to kill one of them, Dad got in our way, and now…

And now Brock was dead.

I couldn't stop shaking. I hadn't even *liked* Brock – he'd been the youngest and weakest and barely useful at best – but that wasn't the point. The fish were alive and he wasn't. Dehaians one, greliarans zero.

"What do we do?" Clay asked Dad. I struggled to keep from hitting him. Who cared what Dad thought? This was his fault as much as anything.

"We get the scale-skins to come to us."

In spite of my anger, my brow furrowed.

Dad turned to Harman. "We want her parents."

The doctor's eyes went wide. I looked between them in confusion. Her parents? Where were her parents in all this?

Dad ignored Harman's alarmed expression. "They'll get her to come back."

"B-but you agreed not to hurt Chloe. I have other experiments–"

"Yes, and you agreed to give us a dehaian. Funny how that worked out."

Harman swallowed again.

Dad paused. "You want more experiments. We can work on that. Bring the girl back and let you have a few days with the boy as well. But we need her parents so we can find them both first."

The doctor's hopes were painted all over his face at the thought of getting another chance to cut into that black-haired fish guy. I scarcely noticed. Dad couldn't be serious. We were going to chase down her parents, and then not even kill the scale-skins when we found them? What kind of plan *was* this?

"Really?" Harman asked.

"You have my word."

I couldn't keep an infuriated noise from escaping.

"B-but won't they know you, though?" the doctor pressed with a nervous glance to me. "From back in Reidsburg, I mean. Won't they know—"

"They never saw us."

Harman swallowed a third time. He seemed to be having trouble stopping. "Okay," he agreed. "Then I'll… I'll tell them you're my other assistants. My ones who deal with dehaians. And that they need to go with you to save their daughter from that Zeke boy. Yeah. They'll believe that."

He shifted his weight, his hands twitching as though he wasn't sure what to do with them. "You won't hurt the girl, though, right? I still need her for—"

"I said you have my word."

Harman gave a tight nod. He hurried back toward the parking lot.

"Dad," I began.

"Shut it."

He strode after Harman.

I stared at them. I could have come up with fifty plans better than this one. A hundred, even. And each of them would have involved tearing both those damn fish to pieces and feeling their magic gush out through the wounds. But instead—

Clay made an irritated sound at me while he moved past, trailing Dad like the pathetic lapdog he was and glaring as if he couldn't understand why I wasn't moving too.

I growled and he dropped the glare. Walking by him, I

followed Dad and Harman into the parking lot. The two of them were heading for the couple by the car, and after a moment, the reason clicked.

Those were her parents.

I walked faster.

"Bill? Linda?" Harman called. "Can we talk?"

The couple paused, caution practically radiating from them.

"These are my assistants," Harman continued. "Richard and his, um, sons."

Bill eyed us, clearly torn about just getting back into the car.

"They can help you find your girl and the… that boy who came with her."

The skepticism on Bill's face didn't fade. "No offense," he said to Dad. "But you all don't look like scientists."

"They're here because of the boy," Harman explained. "To help in case Zeke became… difficult."

Bill's caution abated slightly. "I see."

"They want you to go with them to find Chloe."

The woman, Linda, made a fretfully hopeful noise and hurried around the car. "Do they know where she is?" She looked to Dad. "Have you seen her?"

"We know how to find her," Dad answered.

I glanced to him, realizing what he planned. What I hoped he planned. What, if it'd been me, *I* would've planned.

It was hard to keep the smile from my face.

"Okay," Linda agreed. "Where is she? What do we need to—"

"Just follow us in your car," Dad said.

She rushed for the passenger side of the sedan.

Bill didn't move. "Follow you where?"

Harman fidgeted. "You better go quick, Bill," he urged. "She's in danger. What that boy is capable of…"

The words worked. Bill got in the car.

Dad headed toward our SUV.

"You won't *hurt* anyone, right, Richard?" Harman tried, keeping his voice low while he scuttled after him.

"Make sure the cops don't follow us," Dad told him.

I continued past the doctor when the old man paused. Still clasping his hands, Harman shifted his weight for a moment and then scampered toward the police.

"We actually going to do any of what you told him?" Owen asked.

Wordlessly, Dad tugged open the door and then climbed in. I took the passenger seat, leaving my brothers to get in the back.

"Are we?" Clay pressed.

Dad turned the key in the ignition. "Those ropes still behind you?"

My lip curled. He *did* have the same plan as I would've made.

Dad glanced to us, his expression like ice. "There's a barn about ten miles away. Saw it on our drive here. We pull over, get her parents out, and leave the vehicle there. They'll fit behind you two. But we don't hurt anyone too badly just yet."

"What about that thing you told Harman?" I asked. "How

we'd bring the fish back for him? Not touch the girl?"

Contempt showed on Dad's face as he put the gearshift into drive. "Don't be a moron. We find them, we're killing them all."

❦ 1 ❦

CHLOE

We'd made it almost thirty miles from the warehouse near the Borman Grain company before my parents had tried calling us.

And they hadn't stopped in all the miles since.

"Oh, you have *got* to be kidding," Baylie groaned when the phone buzzed again. She tugged her gaze from the midday traffic on the highway and glanced to Noah. "Could you look this time?"

He pulled open the lid to the center compartment and drew out the cell.

And then returned it to the console without a word.

I sighed. Still my parents then, and not Baylie's stepmom, Sandra, or anyone else. Noah and Baylie continued checking, and kept the phone on vibrate rather than silent just in case their family tried to reach us.

But so far every call had been the same.

"What is that?" he asked tiredly. "Forty?"

"Forty-three," Ellie supplied in a small voice from her seat on the far side of Zeke.

Noah shook his head.

I turned my gaze to the window. Land so flat it could have been ironed surrounded us, though I knew mountains couldn't be much farther ahead. We'd entered Colorado not too long ago, and though the eastern portion of the state was flat enough to seem like Kansas all over again, the western would make all this feel like a weird dream.

Or at least, that's what I remembered from when Zeke and I had driven through an area not too far from here.

The thought made me shift uncomfortably, bringing as it did a hot blush of memory and a nauseated feeling of worry all at the same time. On the seat next to me, Zeke had barely moved over the past several hours. Bandages covered his legs from where Ellie's grandfather had cut him, and bloodstains showed through the gauze. The tendrils of scales that had dangled around the injuries were finally gone, but his skin still glistened in places, as if he could barely keep it from changing. Strange burn marks marred his chest and sides, though both were now covered by the shirt Noah had lent him. I had no idea what Harman had done to him – Zeke hadn't spoken of it during the entire trip – but even all these hours later, he seemed like he'd scarcely gotten better.

I didn't know what to do to help him. We couldn't take him to a hospital – Zeke wasn't human, he had no ID, and Ellie's grandfather or my parents would have the police looking for us besides – and none of us knew of a place to go other than where we were already heading.

But if Ellie's mentor, Olivia, couldn't help him. If he died…

The nauseated feeling grew. Just because *I'd* almost died last night after what that horrible little man had done, that didn't mean Zeke would.

Stomach churning, I pushed the thoughts aside. They weren't helping.

"How much farther?" I asked.

When no one responded, I glanced away from the window.

"A while," Ellie answered apologetically.

My fingers tightened on Zeke's.

He squeezed my hand back.

I let out a breath, trying to allow the small pressure to convince me that everything would be fine.

The phone buzzed.

I closed my eyes.

Time passed and the mountains arrived, swallowing us in shadows even though it was only late afternoon. Cars raced around us, their drivers moving faster for the comfort of not having police looking for them, and the road curved back and forth past slopes that felt surrealistically high.

And the hours crept on.

Stars shone by the time Ellie finally murmured for Baylie to turn off the state highway. The road delivered us into a low-lying city lost between the mountains and bisected by a river cutting a path through its downtown. Tourist traps, all of them long since closed for the night, fronted the waterway, while near the town center, strings of lights glowed around a stage in a park, revealing the trash-and-plastic-cup aftermath of what might've been a concert.

Following Ellie's directions, Baylie steered the car past assorted businesses and the little stands advertising tickets to various events, and into the neighborhoods hiding behind them both. The hilly terrain quickly blocked the lights of the main city street, leaving us winding along dark, narrow roads dotted with houses tucked at odd angles beneath giant trees.

"There," Ellie said, leaning forward a bit to point at a white-walled bungalow nearly lost between two large pines. By the screen door guarding the enclosed porch, a lamp glowed buttery and warm in the darkness, and when we turned into the gravel drive, I could see that the lights at the back of the house were still on as well.

I swallowed hard. I'd known Olivia would be waiting. Ellie had called earlier today to tell her we were coming, and about an hour ago to let her know we were getting close.

But anything could have happened between then and now. Harman could have called and told Olivia what had happened from his perspective. Something else could have changed to put us all in danger. Ellie swore we could trust her mentor, that even though she was a landwalker elder like Harman, Olivia didn't think like him. She wouldn't see me as just a half-and-half kid who needed to be turned back into a landwalker, and she could help with more information about this 'Beast' thing that had caused the Sylphaen to want me dead.

But Ellie could be wrong, and on the roller coaster my life had become, I'd found paranoia of strangers wasn't always the wrong reaction. After all, at least half of them had ended up trying to kill me.

Zeke gently jostled my hand. "It'll be alright," he whispered.

I glanced over, and then caught sight of Noah looking back at us. Discomfort tangled through me for a whole other reason, and hastily, I turned away and pushed open the door.

Warm summer air pressed against me, carrying the smell of pine and river water. The neighborhood was silent, the hour long past when most people probably had gone to bed. From the car, Zeke climbed out. I hesitated, waiting to see if he needed any help.

"I'm fine," he assured me, reading the pause.

I stayed close just in case, and tried to ignore the feeling of Noah watching us both. Ellie led the way while we headed for the porch. The steps creaked beneath us and the hinges of the screen door made popping noises as Ellie pulled it aside. We gathered inside the enclosed porch, and when Ellie knocked, the heavy, mahogany door seemed to absorb the sound.

A second passed and then footsteps hurried toward us from within the house. The door swung open to reveal a slender African-American woman with a short afro and black-framed glasses. Above her jeans, an old flannel shirt covered her, the plaid fabric visibly softened and faded with age. Her dark eyes swept us as though counting and running a calculation on the number she found, and from her face, I couldn't tell what the result could be.

"Hi Olivia," Ellie managed with a tiny, nervous smile. "I'm sorry to drop in so late."

"It's no problem," the woman answered, sounding more cautious than upset. "Is everything okay? You were fairly vague on the phone."

"Uh, yeah. Sorry about that. It's… well, I mean… can we come in?"

Eyebrow twitching up, Olivia nodded. Not looking away from us, she stepped back to allow us all space to enter. Ellie hurried inside, with Baylie coming more slowly behind her. Noah followed, only to pause on the opposite side of the entry from the woman, still watching her. Olivia's eyes skimmed over him questioningly before flicking to us.

And then she spotted the bandages on Zeke's legs. Alarm on her face, she looked to Ellie.

"I can explain that," Ellie began. "It's just… he, uh…"

"Why don't you all join me in the kitchen?" Olivia offered carefully when Ellie trailed off. She waited while Zeke and I walked past her and then she shut the door. "I have a couple chairs in there and I was just getting some cocoa ready."

Ellie took off for the kitchen. Still casting short glances to the wounds on Zeke's legs, Olivia trailed after her.

I took a deep breath to steady myself. With Zeke beside me and Noah a step ahead, I walked down the hall. Through an archway to my left, I could see a darkened study. A trio of monitors sat on the desk in the corner, their blue power lights blinking sleepily. A computer tower waited on the floor near them, and in the dimness, I could make out a thick braid of cables running to additional machines several feet away. Beneath the bay window to the right, a couch sat with a laptop and a few paper file folders on it, the latter of which looked as though they'd been in the middle of being read.

With a wary glance to Olivia, I kept going. At the end of the hallway, a bright glow spilled through the arched entrance. A metal-legged table stood in the middle of the kitchen, while an old, white-enameled gas stove waited to the right with a tea kettle getting ready to whistle on its top.

Olivia crossed to the stovetop and removed the kettle quickly. Turning back, she motioned for us all to take seats around the table. Her ever-present worry still in her eyes, Ellie ghosted over to the cabinets and retrieved a box of instant cocoa and several mugs.

I pulled back a chair, wincing at the scrape of the metal legs across the checkered tile, and then sat down next to Baylie. Zeke and Noah paused, and then Zeke sank into the chair at my side.

The muscles of Noah's jaw jumped. He took a seat next to his stepsister.

I looked away.

"So…" the woman began while Ellie opened a packet of hot chocolate mix. "Like Ellie said, my name is Olivia."

Baylie glanced to me. "I'm Baylie," she replied warily.

"Chloe," I said.

"Noah."

"Zeke."

The woman paused and then cast a quick look to Ellie when nothing more came. "I take it you all had a… well, how was your trip?"

No one answered while Ellie set the mugs down in front of us.

"We need your help," Ellie said.

Olivia waited.

Ellie's gaze twitched to me. "I didn't know what to say on the phone. It's just… things with Grandpa got bad. Complicated bad. He…" She exhaled. "You know how you told me he sometimes can take a hard view on things?"

The woman nodded.

Ellie glanced to us. "He… well, he did. And he, um… he hurt them. Because Chloe and Zeke are dehaians."

Olivia's brow climbed. Her gaze went back to us.

"Well, Zeke, really. And Chloe… she's half-landwalker. But also dehaian. She survived the change."

The woman's brow rose higher as she stared at us. I tried not to fidget under the scrutiny.

"Grandpa tried to take that away from her, though," Ellie continued. "Well, I mean, her parents wanted – her landwalker parents, that is. Sort of. They adopted her. I think that's what Grandpa said. Her mom was the sister of the man who raised her, and then she died so he and his wife adopted her. Or…"

Ellie's tangled explanation failed her and she looked to me.

I hesitated briefly and then nodded.

She exhaled, echoing the motion. "Yeah, so they wanted him to take the dehaian stuff away. But Olivia, she *survived*. She actually *became* one of them."

The woman didn't respond. I couldn't read her expression. Without taking her eyes from me, she accepted a mug of cocoa from Ellie and stood holding it for a long moment in silence.

"You *saw* her change?" Olivia asked Ellie.

My face darkened at the implication.

"Well, she…" Ellie looked to me. "Could you, like, maybe show your, um…?"

She gestured haltingly to my forearms.

I hesitated again before making the spikes come out.

A breath pressed from Olivia's chest. She glanced to Zeke. "And you?"

Zeke didn't respond.

"He's full-blood dehaian," Ellie supplied in a tiny voice. "And Grandpa… he wanted to do testing."

Olivia paused for a heartbeat, and then her gaze returned to me.

I couldn't stop myself from shifting under her study this time. It just didn't seem to end.

"What about your friends?" she asked finally, her focus moving to Baylie and Noah.

From the corner of my eye, I saw Noah tense while Ellie opened her mouth to speak.

"Just friends," I answered.

Ellie closed her mouth, appearing uncomfortable.

I didn't look away from the woman. There wasn't anything particularly important about keeping Noah's greliaran identity a secret – except that if Olivia turned out to be a threat, having someone around whom she'd underestimate might save our lives. She'd already gotten more information from us than we'd gotten from her, and there was no telling what she'd do with it all.

A shiver moved through me. I couldn't believe myself for thinking like this. A few weeks ago, the worst things I had to worry about were jerks at school. But life had changed, and the long drive here had sharpened a few things. I couldn't trust anyone except Noah, Baylie, and Zeke. The jury was still out on Ellie, the fact she'd helped save me after what my parents and Harman had done aside.

But other than that… other than them…

"And him," Olivia continued. "The fact he's here…" Her head leaned toward Zeke, though she didn't look away from me. "That has something to do with you?"

I gave a tight shrug. She exhaled again.

"What else have you been able to do?"

My gaze twitched to Zeke. I didn't know what to say, and I was starting to feel like a circus performer being asked what tricks they knew.

"Look," Noah cut in. "Ellie said you could help us. A whole lot of weird stuff has happened since Chloe found out she was dehaian, and a good chunk of it has tried to kill her. But Ellie said you'd know about it, and maybe even know what we have to do to stop it. So…?"

Olivia's brow drew down. "What kinds of 'stuff'?"

I hesitated and Noah did the same.

"Possessed water," Baylie answered before Noah could speak. "In California. It attacked our boat."

Olivia glanced to Ellie, who shrugged helplessly.

"Did this happen every time you went in the ocean?" Olivia asked me.

I paused. "No."

"Most of the time it just feels like the water is electrified when she's in it," Zeke said. "Though how much varies."

"I don't know what that is," I added before the woman could ask.

Olivia looked away and her dark gaze slid back and forth across the checkered tile as though reading something there.

Ellie fidgeted. "See? And I mean, I've watched the news about the storms hitting the coast and those earthquakes underwater. Olivia, if this is–"

"I'll need to look into it," Olivia interrupted. Her gaze found me again. "But yes. Yes, I'll help you."

Tension seemed to leak out of Ellie, though the woman's words didn't do much for the rest of us.

Harman had thought he was helping me too.

"It's late, though," Olivia continued. "And you…" Her gaze flicked to Zeke again. "You had a long trip. I have an extra room upstairs, and the couch down here isn't bad either. Why don't you all get some rest and we can talk more in the morning?"

A heartbeat passed, and then we pushed our chairs back and rose to our feet. Olivia motioned us toward the hall, and followed when we headed for the stairs.

The ceiling was lower on the second floor, as if it dated from a time when people were shorter, and it made me feel claustrophobic. Olivia directed us to a room at the end of the hall, where we found a queen-sized bed covered in a checkered quilt.

"Bathroom is on the left," Olivia said, "and my room is by the stairs. I'll get some blankets together and then you all can decide who wants to take the couch. Ellie, could you grab the sleeping bag in the closet there? And, um… there should be a second one downstairs somewhere."

Ellie nodded and crossed to the twin folding doors on the left wall of the room. The woman returned to the hall closet, where she set to pulling out blankets and sheets.

I hesitated, and from the corner of my eye, I could see the others do so as well. Reluctance was written all over Baylie's face, along with a fair measure of awkwardness, and in varying degrees, Zeke and Noah's expressions were the same.

"Um… I can take the floor, I guess," Baylie offered.

"That's alright," Noah said.

Her gaze twitched to Zeke. "No, it's fine."

She went to help Olivia before anyone could say anything further.

I bit my lip. Noah and Zeke didn't quite look at each other, and having them both in such proximity was starting to make the air feel like it might explode.

"I'm going to stay up," I told them quietly. "We should probably keep an eye out… you know, in case."

"Chloe," Noah protested. "You need sleep as much as–"

"I've gone longer without it before, and it isn't like I'm tired anyway. It's not a problem."

"That last time wasn't good either," Zeke pointed out in a low voice.

I shifted my weight uncomfortably. "It's not a problem," I repeated.

Without another word, I hurried after Baylie. The last thing I needed was those two ganging up on me, and I didn't want to argue any more than I wanted rest.

After Harman and the Sylphaen and everything else in the past few weeks, I could only too easily imagine the nightmares that were waiting.

In the end, Zeke took the couch.

Tucked in the shadows behind the screen enclosing the porch, I sat on a swing and watched the street. The others were upstairs, asleep most likely, though Noah hadn't looked happy about it. For her part, Baylie hadn't said a word about my plan to stay up. Instead, she'd just given me a weird look, like the news upset her somehow, and then she'd gone to bed.

I'd need to talk to her eventually. There just hadn't been time. Or privacy. Or, on my part, any idea of what to say.

Though she wasn't the only one I needed to talk to.

A moth flew past my face. I waved it off.

It felt pretty crazy, though, sitting out here on watch like some sort of soldier. Odds were, my parents wouldn't figure out where we were and couldn't really pose a threat if they did. I wouldn't let them drag me home again, after all. But then, if the police showed up, or even Harman…

I shook my head, driving the worries away. We could have gone anywhere. They wouldn't just automatically know we were here.

The front door creaked.

I jumped a mile.

Noah hesitated, one hand on the door handle. "Sorry."

Swallowing, I motioned dismissively.

He closed the door behind him and then came over to the porch swing.

A heartbeat passed after he sat down. "You doing okay?" he asked.

I nodded.

Silence fell.

"You?" I asked.

"Yeah."

I couldn't quite bring myself to look at him.

"We should talk, eh?" he tried.

My gaze slid toward him, making it about halfway before giving up. "Yeah, I guess."

A second stretched like a rubber band, ready to snap.

"So… you and that Zeke guy."

My stomach sank.

"How, um… how long's that been going on?"

I hesitated, suddenly feeling as though I'd prefer having Noah's cousins to deal with than this non-conversation. Maybe, anyway.

"Not long."

He was silent at the words.

"After the beach that last time," I managed. "A… a while after that."

I waited, not quite looking at him and feeling like he could see through the lie. It'd been minutes after Noah drove me off, threatening me and saying all sorts of horrible things, that I'd kissed Zeke.

And it'd been an accident.

Though everything since then hadn't been.

"Ah," Noah replied.

My gaze lifted to him.

He was watching the street. "I didn't want to do that. Say… what I said that day. I hated myself for doing that to you. I just–"

"I know."

He glanced back at me. I dropped my gaze to the wood slats of the porch.

"I really thought I was making you safer," he continued. "Even if I didn't want you to go. I'd wanted to see you again. I'd hoped we could, you know…"

He let out a breath, so much more than frustration in the sound.

I couldn't look at him. I knew what he was saying, though, and the realization sent quivers running through me. He'd kissed me the moment before I left for the ocean that first time, and in the days after, I'd wondered what it meant to him, and that maybe it hadn't mattered all that much. I hadn't wanted to get ahead of myself, after all, or make a fool of myself if everything I'd felt hadn't been reality on his side. But I'd wanted to come back and find out if this guy I'd liked for so long actually felt the same way about me.

Now I knew.

"Me too," I whispered.

From the corner of my eye, I saw him turn to look at me.

"And now," he continued. His hand moved over, and I tensed when it brushed mine. "Now, I just want to know if you can forgive me."

Noah's fingertips strayed across the inside of my wrist. I drew a halting breath, my gaze lifting again to his.

"I'm so sorry, Chloe. For all of it. Everything that's come down on you because of me. I'm sorry."

I trembled at the look in his dark green eyes. At the feeling of his hand on my own, and the memory of how he'd held it all those weeks ago when the dehaian stuff was new and the worst thing in the world was finding out I wasn't human.

"Of course I forgive you," I said.

His other hand came up, brushing back my hair from my cheek. Warm shivers ran through me, like electricity that didn't hurt at all.

"I missed you," he continued softly.

I swallowed hard, trying to find my voice. "I missed you too."

He came closer and my gaze fell, tracing the line of his cheek. I could feel his warm breath on my neck, his lips barely an inch from mine.

And my own breath caught. I couldn't do it. Couldn't… not with Zeke asleep in the living room only a few yards from us. I wanted to. I wanted that day when Noah had kissed me back again, and all the days with him that'd come before. I wanted to feel his lips on mine.

But things were so much more complicated now.

I turned away. Out of the corner of my eye, I saw him straighten, his brow furrowing.

"I-I'm sorry," I managed. "I just–"

"No," he said tightly. "Yeah, I…"

I looked back when his hand left mine. He wouldn't meet my eyes.

"I get it," he continued. "I… I'm sorry too."

He hesitated and then pushed to his feet, heading for the door.

"Noah…"

"Goodnight, Chloe."

He disappeared back inside.

It took me a moment to pull my gaze from the door to the empty street. My fingers rested on the place where he'd held my hand, the skin so much colder now for the loss of his touch.

Air pressed from my chest, threatening to turn into a sob, and I fought to keep it from emerging. It wasn't fair. I liked Noah. For years, I'd liked him. But Zeke was wonderful too. There weren't words for the way he made me feel when he looked at me or when he held me in his arms. Both he and Noah were incredible, and I couldn't stop myself from being drawn to either of them any more than I could break the hold of gravity.

My eyes closed as tears burned. It wasn't fair. It just wasn't fair.

And I didn't know what to do.

ZEKE

The shadows of the study were deep, swallowing all but the small lights blinking on the computers nearby. Beneath my back, the sofa sagged in odd places, as though some parts had worn down farther with time than others.

I knew I should sleep. Exhaustion pulled like weights attached to my muscles, driven partly by the unidentifiable drugs that bastard had put in my system, though the dull buzz of pain didn't help either. My legs had stopped the worst of their aching a few hours ago, and my scales had long since been able to turn into skin. But within my arms, phantom pain still pulsed strangely from the spikes that Harman had cut off. I didn't know how it was *possible* for them to hurt – the spikes grew because of magic more than a physical presence beneath our skin – but my body didn't seem to care.

As if responding to my thoughts, a space on my forearm began to ache worse. Distractedly, I rubbed at it.

I hadn't said anything to Chloe about what happened. There wasn't any point. What was done was done, and I didn't want her worrying about me. I was feeling better than I had been, after all, and the spikes would grow back. Eventually, anyway.

And I didn't want to sleep. Chloe was outside alone, nearly invisible in the shadows of the enclosed porch, but alone nonetheless. I couldn't believe anyone had agreed when she'd insisted we go to bed and she stay up doing that. I wasn't about to leave her without someone watching her back, though. There was still a chance one of the innumerable people after her would find out she was here.

I shifted around on the couch and peered through the crack between the curtains. A few yards down the length of the porch, she sat on the swing, her gaze on the darkened street. In the shadows, her auburn hair looked almost black, though her eyes still seemed to catch the light, glinting deep green. She hadn't changed them to see better through the darkness, which made me uncomfortable even if it was probably smart. A person with glowing eyes would attract attention if anyone in the neighborhood happened to glance outside.

But I didn't like her not doing everything she could to stay safe.

A creak sounded from the second floor and my gaze twitched up. Footsteps came closer to the stairs.

I leaned back into the pillows, looking more like I was asleep. I didn't really feel like talking to anybody here, and if that was Olivia and she was proving not to be as willing to help as she and Ellie had claimed…

My eyes closed. The footsteps came down the steps and paused.

I kept my breathing even and worked to stop my remaining spikes from emerging.

The front door opened. Closed.

I opened my eyes.

No one was in the study. I sat up and looked past the curtain again.

It was that Noah guy, sitting down next to Chloe on the swing. His voice was low when he spoke to her, the words indecipherable, and her response was the same. I couldn't see her face – he'd taken the seat on the far side of her, making her turn his way, and all I could see was the edge of him past her hair – but I could read her tension in the way she was sitting.

I made myself draw a breath. He liked her. I wasn't stupid, and it'd take some serious brain trauma not to see that. Everything he'd done to keep his cousins away from her aside, he'd kissed her before she'd left Santa Lucina that first time, and the way he'd been watching her when she wasn't looking made it more than clear that his feelings hadn't changed.

And he knew about things between me and Chloe. That was also obvious.

When it came to that last, though, I didn't really care. Chloe was one of the most incredible people I'd ever met and she'd chosen to be with me.

After what he did to hurt her, anyway.

I pushed the thought aside. That didn't matter. There was no telling how things might have gone if I'd realized earlier what I was feeling for her. For all I knew, this could have started sooner, and what that guy had done wouldn't have changed a thing. I wasn't going to give his actions credit for what I had with Chloe.

And meanwhile, I wanted to be with her. I was going to make *damn* sure I gave her plenty of reasons to still want to be with me.

The guy's hand rose to her face, pushing away her hair. I tensed. A heartbeat passed and he leaned closer.

Shivers coursed through me.

And then she turned away.

I exhaled. I couldn't tell if she'd kissed him. I couldn't tell anything. But a moment later, Noah stood. He hesitated, saying something to her, and then returned to the door.

My attention was locked on Chloe. She seemed upset. Like something had happened, though I wasn't certain which of the two possibilities it was. But she also didn't look elated, or like she'd fallen back into his arms.

I glanced over when the front door closed. In the entryway, Noah paused. His head turned back in Chloe's direction, though the rest of him was still enough to be stone.

He released a breath, the sound of it shaky. And then he looked over at me.

I didn't know if he could see me in the shadows. Much more than the rough shape of me, anyway. From what I could tell, greliarans didn't have the same visual abilities as dehaians, and regardless, his eyes weren't glowing.

I let my own change, bringing him into sharp focus and dispelling the darkness.

His jaw muscles jumped at the sight. I could see the tension in his face, and in the way his hand trembled. His fingers moved, as if he was fighting to keep them from curling into a fist, and then his head twitched toward Chloe again.

He exhaled, short and sharp. A quiver shook him.

Without a word, he turned and climbed the stairs.

I realized I hadn't been breathing, and air filled my lungs quickly. I glanced to Chloe.

She'd looked at the street, but now her eyes were closed. Out in the open, all alone, and her eyes were closed.

Tears glistened on her cheeks.

My hand moved to push the blanket away and then I hesitated. Regardless of what just happened, she probably didn't want me out there. I was itching to go outside, to learn what had passed between her and Noah, and to keep her safe as well, but I wasn't a fool. I knew I had to give her a moment.

Even if I wanted to hurt anything that had hurt her. *Anyone*, for that matter.

I took another breath. I'd talk to her tomorrow. Or in an hour. Or the second she looked like she wouldn't push me away. But in the meantime, I didn't have to leave her unprotected.

My gaze returned to the neighborhood while I shifted around

on the lumpy couch, sitting up to avoid sleep claiming me. I could go another night without rest. Exhaustion be damned, she was distracted right now. And while it was unlikely that her parents or the police would show up, or that the greliaran guy's cousins were anywhere around, unlikely wasn't the same as impossible.

And the loss of a little rest was a tiny price for helping Chloe stay safe.

3

NOAH

I climbed the stairs, fighting with every step not to go back down to the living room and have it out with that dehaian. I didn't know what I planned to say. I wasn't sure *saying* anything was the plan. Shivers rippled through my core, driven by anger and God knew what else, and it was everything I could do to keep my skin from changing.

But I wouldn't be like that. Wouldn't lose control. And pummeling the guy wouldn't fix anything, or endear me to Chloe either.

No matter *how* tempting it was.

I shuddered harder, struggling to keep my greliaran side at bay. Zeke was wary of me, I knew. I'd heard the fact he hadn't breathed till after I left the living room. Some part of me was glad I put him on edge.

The rest of me didn't know what to feel.

My feet stopped at the top of the stairs. On my right,

Olivia's bedroom door was closed and the gap beneath it was dark as if the lights within were off. At the end of the hall, the guest room door stood open, and through it I could see Baylie and Ellie asleep on either side of the large bed. I'd insisted they take it. I wasn't going to make one of them sleep on the floor.

A breath escaped me. It wasn't just kindness to them. I *was* exhausted; I'd barely slept for two days, and the old wizards who'd made us apparently hadn't seen fit to give greliarans the dehaians' ability to stay awake for damn near ever. But I didn't want to sleep, so they might as well have the bed. And tiredness or not, I would've stayed outside with Chloe if she'd wanted me to be there. I refused to leave her to keep watch by herself. Not when she was the target in all this – more than the rest of us, anyway – and when, in this quiet, I could hear a good chunk of the neighborhood if I tried. I'd probably know if anyone was heading our way long before they came into view.

At least, I hoped.

But regardless, I didn't want to sleep.

I crossed to the tiny window on the opposite wall from the stairwell. The street was dark, with only a few porch lamps to break the blackness, though most of the lights just caught on the large pines near the houses and created deep pools of shadow on the trees' other sides. Wisps of clouds drifted through the sky, hazing over the stars and veiling the moon, and through the cracks around the old window frame, I could catch whiffs of evergreen on the night air.

My hand curled into a fist and my arm rested above my

head on the wall, bracing me beside the window. I'd needed to go out there. I'd needed to talk to her and know for certain what was between her and that guy. I mean, I'd been pretty sure. It was practically written all over them.

But I'd still needed to hear it from her.

And now…

My arm trembled with the urge to hit the wall.

Truthfully, it wasn't this guy that bothered me. Not really. Or, maybe just not *entirely*. I hated the sight of him, yes, and would *happily* chuck him into the nearest body of water and leave him there to rot, but that wasn't the point. He'd been there. He'd probably comforted her, and talked to her, and made her feel safe. And I hadn't. Instead, I'd been the one to hurt her. To drive her away. It didn't matter that I hadn't had much of a choice at the time. Or that my cousins would have killed her. Or that there hadn't been any opportunity to explain.

It didn't change what I'd done.

So it made sense she'd looked elsewhere after what happened. I got that. I *hated* it, but I got it. I just didn't want to leave things that way. I wanted a chance to fix this. To make it up to her and get back to what we'd started to have before those dehaian bastards drugged her and she'd been forced to leave.

And punching Zeke wouldn't do that. Probably not, anyway.

Grimacing, I scrubbed my other hand over my face, ordering myself to stay awake and focus. I'd figure something out—something that didn't involve breaking the face of that dehaian.

I'd get her back, and I'd do my *damnedest* never to hurt her again.

I wasn't going to let things between me and Chloe end like this.

4

CHLOE

It was strange how, even when you'd been watching the darkness all night, sunrise could still take you by surprise. One minute, the sky was dark, and the next, you realized the world was easier to see.

Though maybe I was just distracted. I had, after all, spent the entire night torn between the desire to pace furiously and the impulse to cry about the stupid, complicated mess my life had become.

Drawing a shaky breath, I attempted to focus back on the street. Nothing had happened all night long, barring a few stray cats wandering through the darkness and the occasional cry of some wild animal. Within the past several minutes, curtains had started to pull back on the windows of houses along the street, the early risers letting the barest hints of morning light into their homes while they got ready for the day. But that was all.

The front door opened, breaking the stillness. Baylie stuck

her head outside.

She paused at the sight of me. "Hey."

"Hey."

"You're still up," she said, awkwardly stating the obvious.

I nodded.

"You doing alright?"

"Uh-huh."

Baylie hesitated and then came the rest of the way onto the porch. Wordlessly, she crossed to the swing and sat down.

A moment passed.

"Noah told me you don't... you don't need to sleep anymore."

I tried not to fidget uncomfortably. I wasn't sure what to say.

"But you used to, right? I mean..." She looked uneasy.

"Yeah."

At the tension in my tone, she grimaced. "I'm sorry. It's just–"

"Weird."

"Freaky."

I couldn't stop myself from shifting on the seat this time.

Out of nowhere, she gave a scoffing chuckle. I glanced to her, confused.

"Sorry," she explained. "Noah... when I found out about him, he said that, and then I answered sort of the same way and I just..." The chuckle came again, the sound a bit more strained. "Yeah."

I wasn't sure how to respond.

Running a hand through her blonde hair, she let out a breath. "So what's it like?" she asked, a lighter note in her voice. "Underwater, I mean."

I studied her warily. "It's alright."

Her face took on a dry expression.

My caution didn't fade. "Are you really okay about all this?"

"I'm going to be."

My brow twitched up. She sighed.

"Chloe, you've been my friend since forever. And now you're part… that. It's taking some getting used to. But I will. I *promise* I will." She shrugged. "Anyway, I'd pretty much suck if I dumped our friendship over it, wouldn't I?"

Incredulity bubbled up and I gave a choked laugh.

She echoed the sound and then reached out, putting her arms around me. I squeezed her tight into a hug, tears stinging my eyes.

"Just don't stab me with those spiky things, eh?" she warned.

My breath caught and I straightened. "I wouldn't. I have to want them to–"

"I was joking," she told me with a flat look.

I managed a jerky nod. Her eyes took on a sympathetic cast.

"Freaky, huh?" she said quietly.

"Takes some getting used to."

Her lip twitched. "What's it like in the ocean?"

I shrugged. "It's okay. I mean, it's strange. Like… they have a whole world down there. Cities, countries, royalty…" I glanced back to the living room, uncertain if I should tell her about Zeke.

"Wow," Baylie said.

I blinked, my focus returning to her. "Yeah."

She looked away.

I hesitated, catching something in her expression. "What?"

Baylie shook her head. "Nothing. Just… sounds interesting." She drew a breath. "You miss it?"

I paused. I hadn't really thought about it. There hadn't been much chance, what with everything that'd happened since. "I guess."

Her brow rose. "You guess? Come on, you *always* wanted to go to the ocean, Chloe. How could you not find this awesome? I mean, who doesn't want to…" She hesitated. "You know, breathe underwater and all that."

I looked down. I'd wanted to visit the ocean since I was a kid, it was true. But my body changing like it did still seemed bizarre, at least when I was up here on land and almost no one else was like me.

"I just think it'd be cool," Baylie finished.

I glanced to her and spotted that expression again, only this time I realized what it was.

She wanted to go there. See those things.

And she couldn't.

I swallowed. "It has its downsides," I tried. "Sharks… cults… mercenaries who tried to kill us."

"Mercenaries who tried to kill you," she repeated. "Why?"

I hesitated. "Long story."

She blinked, looking away. "Well, besides that, then. Cool otherwise."

A moment passed.

"So… that Zeke guy."

I tensed. "What about him?"

"He–"

The door opened. Ellie leaned her head out.

"Um, could you all come inside?" she asked. "Olivia wants to talk."

It took me a second to regroup. "Yeah, alright."

Ellie hesitated and then disappeared back into the house.

"Nervous little thing, isn't she?" Baylie commented quietly.

I glanced over. "You trust her?"

Baylie seemed surprised by the question. "I guess. I mean, she did help us get you and Zeke away from her grandfather."

I looked down, nodding. I knew that, just like I knew I should probably let it be enough to convince me she was okay.

But Niall had seemed trustworthy too, right up until the moment he turned on us.

"Come on," Baylie said, rising to her feet.

I nodded again. Working to push the thoughts aside, I followed her into the house.

In the study, Zeke was sitting on the couch, looking no more rested than yesterday. "Morning," he said with a nod when we came in.

I paused. "You sleep?"

He glanced to the window. "I–"

Noah came down the stairs.

"Hey," Baylie said to him. "I thought I told you to get some rest."

Awkward hesitation flashed over Noah's face.

My own expression wasn't much different. They'd both stayed up. The dark circles under their eyes were more than enough evidence of that. And from what I knew of them, I could guess what they'd been doing – each keeping an eye on the neighborhood with me, albeit from different places in the house.

The thought just made the awkwardness worse. Not knowing what else to do, I fled toward the kitchen.

I couldn't stifle a breath of relief when Baylie was the only one who followed me.

Over the stovetop, Olivia was scrambling eggs in a cast iron skillet, while Ellie was filling glasses with orange juice. The worry hadn't left the girl's expression – I was starting to suspect it never did – and her lip slipped between her teeth when we came in.

"Good morning," Baylie allowed with a wary look to the girl.

"Hi there," Olivia replied, smiling.

"Anything we can help with?" Baylie asked.

"Oh, no, that's fine. Just have a seat. This'll be ready in a second." She paused, glancing to me. "If you want food, that is?"

I froze, my hand on the chair to pull it away from the table. I could see Baylie's incredulous expression from the corner of my eye. Discomfort increasing by the moment, I kept myself from looking to her.

"Yeah, sure," I answered while I finished sitting down. "Thanks."

Olivia smiled again. "I wasn't sure if the distance from the water affected that. Made you need to eat on a more human schedule, I mean. What about sleep? Did you need that at all last night?"

I hesitated again. "Not really."

She glanced back, and from her face, she must have caught something in my expression. "I'm sorry," she said, chagrinned. "I don't mean to bombard you with questions."

"Zeke knows more about this stuff than me."

She scooped the scrambled eggs onto two plates. "Zeke's not half-landwalker, though. He's never been like a human."

I tensed, the words reminding me of the prejudices my parents had against dehaians. The way they'd called dehaians soulless creatures and murderers. "What's that supposed to mean?"

Olivia's brow drew down at the tone. "Just that he wouldn't know what it's like to need food or sleep every day, or to have to worry about not seeing in the dark. That sort of thing."

She gave a shrug as though she couldn't understand my caution.

"Oh," I managed, feeling Baylie watching me.

Olivia set the plates in front of us. Ellie ghosted after her, placing the glasses nearby.

I studied the eggs, suddenly wondering if I should trust the food. People had tried to drug us before…

"Are you okay?" Baylie asked, a touch of caution in her voice.

I glanced to her. She was eyeing Ellie.

The girl swallowed. "Grandpa started calling this morning."

I tensed all over again.

"Did you answer the phone?" Baylie continued.

Ellie shook her head hurriedly.

Baylie let out a breath. Ellie's face tightened like she agreed with the sentiment and then she returned to the counter to get her own juice.

"Your parents haven't stopped trying to reach us either," Baylie told me in a low voice.

I grimaced.

Silence fell as Ellie and Olivia came back to the table. Their forks clinked against their plates and, seeing them eating the food, I started in as well.

This paranoia was as strange as everything else that'd changed in my life.

But recognizing that didn't make the fear go away.

My stomach twisting with nervous energy, I stuck the fork into another bite of the scrambled eggs.

"So Ellie said you wanted to talk to us?" Baylie prompted Olivia after a moment. "Was it about the food thing?"

I could hear the hesitation in her voice, but Olivia just shook her head.

"No," she answered with a smile. "Like I said, I have so many questions, but that can come later. At the moment, I wanted to talk about what I can do to help you."

I waited, still cautious.

"Ellie told you I'm one of the landwalker elders, right?"

I nodded.

"There are about fifty of us, and I can assure you," she glanced to Ellie with a hint of an apologetic look, "we're not all like Doctor Brooks. Before you came in, Ellie was sharing a bit more of what happened to you and Zeke while you were in Iowa, and all I can say is that I'm sorry. I respect Ellie's grandfather for the work he's done on behalf of those few half-and-half kids who've been born in the past several decades, and I know that to some extent, he was just doing as your parents asked. But for the other things…"

I fought to keep from shifting in the seat. I didn't want to remember.

She seemed to see my discomfort. Her apologetic expression strengthened. "We don't all think like him. And with a decent amount of certainty, I can tell you that if – *when* – the others who feel as I do learn about what happened… they won't be pleased."

I returned my gaze to the plate, unsure what to say to that.

"So how can you help?" Baylie asked.

Olivia sighed. "Well, like I said, I'll be telling them what happened, but telling them isn't enough. How old are you, Chloe?"

My brow furrowed warily. "Seventeen."

Olivia nodded as though she'd expected the answer. "So you're a minor in the eyes of the law, which means that your parents still have legal claim over you. And after what they did – and given the connections that Harman has – there is the possibility that they will attempt to bring you home with them and expose you to the treatments a second time."

I shivered. There was more than a 'possibility'. A lot more. Mom and Dad wouldn't listen to me – to anyone – when we told them that I'd almost died from those 'treatments'. They'd just believe that they knew best and wait for their opportunity to try again.

"So this is where the elders need to help you," Olivia continued. "You're special, Chloe. Unlike any half-landwalker, half-dehaian person born in… well, our history. You've survived changing into a dehaian, you've come back on land all this way and even brought a full-blood dehaian with you. And while, yes, I'd say that needs to be studied, I don't mean the way Harman would. And I don't mean right now. At the moment, we have bigger concerns.

"Ellie said she told you about the story of a creature called the Beast."

"A bit," I allowed.

"I realize that must sound preposterous, and I thank you for not deciding we are all lunatics and leaving at your first opportunity."

Olivia smiled. I tried not to grimace, uncertain if I should mention the Sylphaen. Or if I should give her any extra information about my life at all.

"This creature is drawn by someone like you. From everything we know, the Beast is more a force than a physical being, and it feeds on certain kinds of magic – including that of the original dehaians. Thus, those original dehaians divided their abilities, leaving one side without magic in the traditional sense and trapped on land, while the other had magic but was trapped in the ocean. And this worked. It took years for this splitting to fully drain the Beast of energy, but eventually, the creature faded into virtual nonexistence.

"Until you.

"Even the tiniest bit of magic like the original dehaians was enough to start the Beast waking again. And now it's returning. So this is why we need the other elders' help. We need to figure out what to do about this – and soon, before the Beast becomes any stronger. And we need to protect you in the process."

"Why should I trust you?" I asked quietly.

She smiled again, as though she'd expected the question. "Because, at the moment, I wonder if you have a better option. The landwalker elders are incredibly connected. We have many options at our disposal to help you, in the legal sphere and beyond. But Harman will try to use his connections in order to get you back, for his own reasons and possibly on behalf of your parents. I imagine he's already started working toward finding you and Zeke again. Yet I'd hazard a guess that you can't simply return to the ocean. Even if that didn't stand a chance of strengthening the Beast, I assume you left for a reason. And I have gotten the impression," her gaze flicked over me and Baylie, "that reason was not homesickness."

I didn't respond.

"You can try to stay away from them, Chloe, but the police watch for runaways and they *will* bring you home to your parents eventually. Additionally, you were recently reported as the victim of a kidnapping, correct? That news was passed around among the elders, even before the police chief in your town told us you had come home. We watch out for our own, even if their parents have cut ties with us to a great degree. But technically 'found' or not, the point remains you will be viewed as the victim of a crime. The police will be even more motivated to question you and then return you to your parents as a result. However, if you allow us, the elders who value life and knowledge as I do will make certain that does not happen. You're too valuable to us, and the threat of the Beast is too real."

"But you want this Beast thing gone too, right?" Baylie cut in, her voice hard. "Why should we trust you won't just kill her to make that happen?"

My gaze twitched to Baylie, grateful for her question even if I was surprised she'd asked it.

I thought I was the only one finding themselves thinking in that extreme of terms.

"Because it wouldn't work," Olivia answered patiently. "And because it would be a terrible idea – ethically as well as logically.

Magic… it's energy, but it is also unique in the world. It can take forms, can affect physical things, much like it causes Chloe's body to change shape. But when a person with magic is killed, my understanding based on our research is that their death triggers a release of that energy – which, in Chloe's case, would essentially be giving the Beast an influx of exactly what it needs to grow stronger."

I swallowed. The Sylphaen wanted to kill me. Thought that they could take what I was and make themselves that way. They thought it would defeat the Beast or at least give them a chance to fight it.

And now I could see how they thought that was possible. At least the 'taking what I was' part. If they killed me, if this magical energy thing was released when I died and they knew how to capture that and use it for themselves somehow…

I shuddered. This was madness. My whole life had become madness. And the Sylphaen were mad too. If they did what they planned, it'd just bring this Beast thing back faster.

The urge to run rose up again for the first time in a while, though I knew there still wasn't anywhere to go.

"Plus," Ellie added quietly, "if the elders kill Chloe, the landwalkers would never stand a chance of getting our dehaian sides back. It'd be over. By helping her, maybe we can figure out how to become dehaian again and keep the Beast from coming back at the same time."

Olivia glanced to Ellie, a tinge of pity flashing through her eyes and then swiftly buried.

"There are numerous reasons to help Chloe survive," the woman said, "so please, know that we are not out to harm you."

I hesitated. I wished Noah and Zeke were in here. I wasn't sure why Olivia hadn't asked them to come for breakfast, except perhaps she'd noticed they hadn't slept. She seemed decently observant – creepily so, actually. And maybe Noah was listening, if he hadn't fallen asleep yet.

It would have been nice to have more people that I trusted around me right now.

"No." Baylie set down her drink. "No, we're not going to them. We know about these elders, and about their 'connections'. We know what you guys have really been up to."

Olivia's brow drew down. "I'm not sure I understand you."

"The greliarans."

"Greliarans?" Olivia looked to Ellie, who wouldn't meet her eyes. "How do you know about greliarans?"

"Doesn't matter," Baylie replied. "We know you all made a deal with them. That in exchange for capturing people like her," she twitched her head toward me, "you offered to let the greliarans kill them after you got done experimenting. We're not taking her anywhere – or Zeke either – just so you guys can treat them like lab rats and give them up to the greliarans when you're done."

Olivia stared at her. "I don't know what you heard, but we have no such deal. Greliarans are animals. They're barely capable of being in the human world – at best, they're barely even *sane*."

Baylie's face darkened.

At her anger, Olivia paused, a quizzical look in her eyes. "Now, I will admit," the woman allowed, "that all those things aside, we *have* worked in favor of the greliarans in the past. We decided long ago that it was best to keep them contained on the coast. They don't seem to react to us the way they do with dehaians, but that doesn't mean we're interested in having them around. Desperation could still drive them to try killing us. And they seem to prefer the area anyway. As such, we've used our influence to get zoning decisions in their favor, keeping them isolated and preventing humans from coming near their homes, and we've agreed to clean up minor crimes when their tendencies get the better of them. We've even helped those that *do* end up in prison by making certain they are isolated so their secret does not come out, all in exchange for their agreement to stay in coastal areas and away from us. That arrangement could be seen as regrettable and on some level, I would rather we had never created it, but," she shook her head, "that's still a *far* cry from what you're talking about."

"You're lying," Baylie countered.

"I assure you, I'm not." Olivia's hands moved in a short shrug, as though questioning why we were talking about this. "Dehaians almost never make it far enough inland to be in a place where landwalkers could meet them, and even if they do, they're seldom in the best shape by the time that happens. It's why children like Chloe are so rare to begin with. Only *incredibly* resilient people of either lineage can reach a location where they can be in contact for very long without one or the other of them subsequently needing to be hospitalized. And that's the best case scenario. For someone to think they could make a deal with greliarans to bring dehaians *anywhere*, let alone here…"

She trailed off, shaking her head again as though it was too absurd to be believed.

"Zeke heard them," I said. "Ask him."

Olivia watched me, still seeming incredulous. I waited.

"I will," she agreed after a moment. She glanced to Ellie. "But even if Harman was so misguided as to think that was possible, it doesn't mean the rest of us have a similar arrangement. We don't."

"Maybe just some of you don't," I said quietly.

Olivia paused. "You can trust us. The elders I know, the ones to whom I want to take you… they would *never* agree to what you're describing. I swear."

I glanced to Baylie. It was still a risk.

But I didn't know what else we could do. Olivia was still right, about Harman and my parents if nothing else. They wouldn't stop trying to get me back. There was no chance they wouldn't want to put me through those treatments again.

And meanwhile, Zeke's family was still out there with that Beast thing on its way.

"Alright," I agreed. "We'll go meet them."

Olivia nodded and then rose, heading for the phone.

I closed my eyes, hoping desperately that I wasn't making a mistake.

With the dishes delivered to the sink, Baylie and I headed back down the hall. On the couch in the study, Zeke appeared to be asleep and, rather than risk waking Noah if he was the same upstairs, we returned to the porch and sat down on the swing.

I scanned the neighborhood, noting that most of the homes still had cars in the driveways. But then, maybe it was the weekend. I couldn't know. I barely remembered the month anymore, let alone the day. I was so out of touch with everything, it was laughable.

And now some woman I'd just met was going to take me to a secret society that hopefully could stop what I was from destroying the world.

Really, laughable didn't even come close.

"Chloe?"

"Huh?"

I glanced over to find Baylie studying me.

"You didn't hear a word I just said, did you?"

I ran the past few seconds through my mind and came up blank. I winced. "Sorry."

She sighed. "I asked if you were sure about this. And I'm going to guess that's a no."

I shook my head. "Not really. But I don't know what else to do."

"We could come up with something. I know we could.

Something that'd keep your parents away and that Beast thing too. We don't have to go–"

"We can't just run away, Baylie. I mean…"

I looked down. The problem was the same as it had always been – where would I go? I couldn't return to the ocean; the Sylphaen would find me, and that was if that Beast thing didn't get there first. I couldn't take off on land either. Olivia was right; I'd surely run into a cop sooner or later, and they'd only try to force me go home.

And meanwhile, Baylie had a life. We'd joked about running away together when we were little, but that's what kids did. It bore no connection to reality. She couldn't simply go be homeless with me for however long it took this mess to end.

"There aren't really any options," I said.

Baylie grimaced. "Maybe not *many*, but that doesn't mean–"

The door opened and she cut off.

"You guys alright?" Ellie asked.

I nodded.

With a glance to the house, Ellie stepped outside and then shut the door behind her. "Listen, I just wanted to say I think you're doing the right thing. Olivia can help."

I didn't answer. Biting her lip, Ellie hesitated and then sank down on the porch. Leaning back against the rails, she drew her legs up, hugging them close.

"You okay?" I asked.

She nodded.

I waited, but nothing else came.

"You didn't tell her about Noah," I said, a question in the statement somewhere.

She shifted position. "Well, he…" Her gaze twitched back to the house and a weird look flashed over her face, almost like a tremulous smile, swiftly smothered when she dropped her gaze to her knees. "Secrets, right?" she finished with a tiny shrug. "It's not mine."

Baylie's eyebrows rose slightly. "Well, um… okay."

"Thanks," I added.

Ellie nodded again, not looking up at us.

I glanced to Baylie. Her brow hadn't come back down.

And my own expression probably wasn't too different. Ellie liked Noah.

I wondered if he knew.

"So," Baylie tried. "Where are these people Olivia wants us to meet?"

"She's setting up a place," Ellie said, giving no sign she'd noticed our surprise. "Probably her office. They're scattered, though. It'll take a few hours for them to get here."

"Office?"

Ellie shrugged at Baylie's question. "She's an insurance broker. She's got an office close to downtown."

I paused. I'd always associated insurance salespeople with being only slightly less scaly than snakes. After all, the one insurance guy in Reidsburg had always looked like he had some kind of profit-sharing deal with the used car salesman next door.

Olivia didn't seem like that at all.

At least, I hoped.

"What do you know about them?" I asked.

Ellie hesitated. "Not a *huge* amount," she allowed awkwardly. "Like I said, the elders are kind of scattered. They want it that way so, if anything happens like a fire or whatever, we don't lose all the stuff from our history. The stuff that can't be put on computers, anyway. But I mostly work with Olivia. I only started helping Grandpa this summer, and I've met just a few of the others. They don't get together more than a couple times a year in person, and usually just talk online using code language and other stuff that… well, that Olivia hasn't really taught me a lot of yet."

I tried not to grimace. That didn't exactly fill me with confidence.

"How'd you get involved in this, anyway?" Baylie asked. "Is it like a family thing?"

Ellie nodded. "More or less, yeah. I mean, if they think you're smart enough and teachable enough to be worth the time to train, then it is. Mom and Dad could have been elders, easy. They just weren't into it. Mom prefers teaching and Dad loves his job as a programmer, so…" She shrugged. "But we'd visit Grandpa for the holidays and the two of us would spend hours talking about history or looking at all the cool things in his study…" She seemed embarrassed. "You probably think I'm a total dork."

"No," Baylie assured her. "Of course we don't."

I made a noise of agreement. I was the kid with the psycho parents who'd grounded her for coming near a yard sprinkler, and I could count on one hand the times I'd had an actual *conversation* with my mom or dad – since in my book, lectures and arguments and screaming matches didn't exactly count.

Ellie's childhood sounded great from my perspective.

"Okay," Ellie said, a shy smile hovering around her mouth. "But yeah, the elder stuff is mostly a family thing. I just work with Olivia because she lives closer to us than Grandpa. Her grandmother was an elder, though, and Grandpa's uncle trained him. Your mentor keeps teaching you till they think you're ready and… and sometimes that can take a while."

My brow flickered down at the hint of discomfort in her tone.

The door to the house opened again. Olivia stuck her head outside.

"Ellie, your parents are on the phone. They'd like to speak with you." She paused. "I get the impression your grandfather's been calling them."

"You think he knows we're here?" I asked, tensing.

"Probably not for certain," Olivia allowed. "Though I suspect he'll think of it." She returned her gaze to Ellie. "But your mom and dad are worried. They say they've been trying to reach you."

The girl grimaced. "I was going to call…"

"Talk to them now. And you two," she looked to me and Baylie, "wake your friends. We're going to meet several of the others outside town. Harman knows where my office is located, so that's not the safest place. We'll head out in a few minutes so that if anyone *does* come looking, they won't find you regardless."

I swallowed. I didn't want to think about the greliarans or who-knew-what-else coming after us again. I'd be happy if they all just stayed on the other side of the country forever. Or the world.

"Alright," I agreed with a jerky nod.

Olivia ducked back inside. Ellie climbed to her feet and followed.

I glanced to Baylie, seeing the same tension on her face that I could feel on my own.

"I'll go wake up Noah," she said tightly.

"Thanks."

We rose and headed into the house, the bright summer day feeling so much more threatening than before.

5

ZEKE

Consciousness returned at the feeling of a hand shaking me. I tried not to groan. I couldn't have been out for very long. Everything in my body was still attempting to drag me back down to sleep like I was wrapped in anchor chains.

Blinking tiredly, I looked over to find Chloe crouched beside me.

"Hey," I said, a smile spreading over my face as my exhaustion quickly became second in my priorities.

My hand reached from beneath the blankets to slide around her waist.

She tensed. "Hey," she answered, pulling back a bit.

I stopped. Confused, I glanced around the room, noting that Noah was nowhere to be seen.

And yet she still didn't want me to touch her. That wasn't exactly a good sign.

"What is it?" I asked cautiously, pushing away from the cushions to rest my weight on an elbow.

"Olivia thinks Harman will figure out we're here. She wants us to pack up and leave with her, so if he or the greliarans come by, they won't find us."

My brow climbed.

"Yeah," she said, glancing up briefly to catch my expression.

She moved away from the couch, giving me room.

I pushed the blankets aside and stood. "Does she know how soon they might be here?"

Chloe shook her head.

I paused. She wasn't quite looking at me and her gaze kept twitching to the hall.

"Chloe, I–"

The sound of footsteps cut me off. I looked up to see Noah coming down the stairs after Baylie. He appeared exhausted too, and he was blinking as if trying to clear the sleep from his eyes.

With an aborted glance to him, Chloe retreated toward the kitchen.

I saw him hesitate, watching her. Keeping myself from scowling, I followed her and, a heartbeat later, heard Noah do the same.

By a kitchen counter, Olivia was zipping up a blue cooler bag. In the corner, Ellie stood clutching the phone to her ear, more nervousness on her face than normal.

Which was saying something.

"So have any of you been to Colorado before?" Olivia asked with a smile when we came in.

I shook my head and the others did the same.

"We're going to take the Midnight Cave trail just outside town. It's closed right now – rockslide damage – but one of the rangers owes me a favor. It'll make a good place to meet the others where we won't be disturbed."

"Sounds nice," Baylie offered when no one else replied.

Ellie hung up the phone.

"Everything alright?" Chloe asked.

The girl paused. "He… he *is* coming here. One of his assistants is driving him."

Chloe's skin seemed to lose any trace of color. I reached out, putting a hand to her back.

She flinched and her head twitched toward me. Her face tightened, that same unwilling look flashing through her eyes.

I hesitated and then let my hand drop away.

"He told my parents we had a fight," Ellie continued. "They want me to come home."

Olivia nodded. "That's fine. You probably should."

Ellie's brow furrowed with hurt. "But–"

"Actually," Chloe interrupted, a strange expression on her face. "If it's okay with you, I'd prefer Ellie come with us."

Olivia paused.

"She can spot the greliarans working with her grandfather," Chloe continued, not taking her eyes from the woman.

Olivia made a hedging noise. "There's really no need. If I don't recognize someone who comes to the meeting–"

"Please."

The woman hesitated again and then nodded. "Call them back," she said to Ellie. "Tell them I have a bit of training for you today and you'll be home soon."

Ellie nodded quickly. With a grateful glance to Chloe, she hurried to the phone.

Chloe didn't look away from Olivia.

The woman picked up the cooler bag and then slung it over her shoulder, not seeming to notice the attention. "So, could you all follow in your car?"

"Sure," Baylie replied.

Olivia headed for the door.

"What was that about?" Baylie asked Chloe in a low voice.

Chloe pulled her gaze from Olivia. "It's just… Ellie'll know better if something's wrong." She glanced to me. "Like she did with her grandfather."

I paused, remembering how uncomfortable Ellie had been at Harman's house, even compared to her normal anxiousness. She'd known what they were going to do to us. She'd attempted to argue against it.

"And I'm not sure I trust Olivia yet," Chloe finished.

Baylie nodded. "Yeah."

Ellie hung up the phone. A smile spread across her face as she came back over to us.

"Thank you," she said to Chloe. "I know they're worried, but I'd really like to do what I can to help you guys."

"No problem," Chloe said.

The girl's smile grew. She hurried for the door.

Chloe and Baylie shared a glance, their cautious expressions nearly identical, and then they headed after Olivia as well.

I followed them, ignoring Noah. I didn't know what'd happened in the short time I'd been asleep, but even more than before, Chloe looked on edge.

And like so much else, that couldn't be a good sign.

6

WYATT

We'd burned through the charge in the cell phone twice and still we hadn't reached the damn fish.

Clay muttered a curse and hung up. "You *sure* we can't just leave a fucking message?"

"Keep calling," Dad ordered from behind the wheel. "I want to hear her voice when we tell her."

I kept my eyes on the view beyond the window. We'd been meandering across Wyoming for most of the night, stopping occasionally and generally buying time till the girl finally picked up the line. Dad didn't want to push it, or take the landwalkers too close to the coast before the girl knew what was happening. It was no good killing them with proximity to the water if the girl wasn't even aware we were doing it.

Though at least it'd make her father shut up.

I grimaced as the woman began crying again. I didn't mind the sound. There was something soothing about things being afraid of you, like a certain rightness to the universe. But the

guy would start comforting her, and his whispers of how everything would be alright annoyed the hell out of me. He seriously
thought they both weren't dead in all this. That by keeping her
quiet, rather than ditching her and gnawing his own leg off like
some animal in a trap, he still stood a chance of surviving and
the woman did too.

It was revolting.

His little whispers started up again. I pressed my head to the
window glass. Much more of this, and those two wouldn't make
it to Washington – to hell with the plan. Dad's idea was to get
a hold of the fish girl, tell her to meet us at our cabin or else,
and then head back home and wait for her. I wasn't sure which
of us he intended to let have the girl – though I was pretty
certain he wanted to kill that black-haired bastard himself after
what the guy did to Brock – but if Clay or Owen thought they
were going to get a chance at her, they were sorely mistaken. I
was the oldest. I'd been waiting the longest. I was damn well
going to be the one to take that girl's life, and if either of them
got in the way, I'd just have one more body to bury.

Though all that was irrelevant if we couldn't get a teenager
to answer her fucking phone.

"This plan blows," I muttered.

"You got a better one?" Dad snapped.

I paused. I probably shouldn't have said that out loud. He
sounded pissed.

And I didn't have an answer anyway. I'd kill her father and
leave his body for the cops, under the assumption that the bitch

would hear about it eventually, but Dad probably wouldn't agree. More leverage was better and all that.

But at least I wouldn't have to listen to the guy anymore.

"We could try Harman?" Clay suggested from the back seat. "See if he knows any other numbers to call?"

Disgust twisted my face. "That little weasel won't–"

"Good idea," Dad said. "Call him."

I could have punched Clay for his smirk.

Knowing I couldn't easily reach him over the seat, he ignored my glare while he thumbed on the phone and then dialed. "It's us," he said when the doctor answered. "We can't reach the fish. Who else can we call?"

My ears picked up the sound of Harman sputtering.

"I-I think she might've headed to Fort Pedrosa. My granddaughter… she's with them and so we're–"

The sounds were muffled for a moment as Dad reached back. "Give me that."

Clay handed the phone over.

"Why the hell didn't you tell us this earlier?" Dad demanded.

"Well, I mean, I wasn't… Eleanor's a very smart girl. She *might* go there, but…" Harman seemed to regroup. "It's under control, Richard. I have the chief of police from Chloe's hometown with me. He understands the seriousness of this and of what that dehaian boy has done. Don't worry; we're only minutes away from Fort Pedrosa and if we find Chloe and Zeke there, Barry will help–"

"We don't need *help*," Dad growled. "Give us your

granddaughter's number."

Harman was quiet for a moment. "Now, Richard, Eleanor is my–"

"You want the fish or not?"

The old man listed off the number. I smiled.

"You understand, though," Harman continued. "Eleanor isn't to be–"

Dad hung up.

"We going to that place?" Owen asked.

"No."

Dad extended the phone to me. "Call the granddaughter."

My brow climbed. "What? We're still–"

"Weren't you listening?" Dad snapped. "They might not be there. I'm not chasing them to Colorado just to find out those scum-suckers are somewhere else. We're getting them to come to us this time, no matter what."

I made no move to take the cell, my expression unchanged.

Giving me a disgusted look, Dad tossed the phone back to Clay.

"Call her," he ordered again.

Clay dialed the number.

I turned to the window. This was stupid. No, it was beyond stupid. It was driving in *circles*. We'd been at this for a day already and we'd be at it for more, the way Dad was handling things. If the fish was somewhere, even if there was a *chance* the fish was somewhere, we should head to that place.

That's what hunting *was*.

My gaze slid to Dad. He wasn't watching me anymore, and his hands moved on the steering wheel like he was imagining wrapping his fingers around that guy's throat.

I would've come up with *so* many better plans than this. I'd have the fish already and Brock… well, dead or not, whatever. But we'd have the fish. We wouldn't be just driving around like a bunch of old ladies lost in the countryside.

The woman started up crying again and the man whispered stupid words of comfort like he couldn't see the reality in front of his eyes. I rested my head back on the glass. This would change soon. Whether by the girl answering the phone or my patience coming to an end, this would change.

I'd make sure of it.

$$\mathcal{C} \sim 7 \sim \mathcal{O}$$

NOAH

The scents of pine and mulch surrounded us, and so many birds filled the trees with their cries that I felt like I was being bombarded by a Hollywood sound effect. The trail ahead of us curved through the forest, as did the one behind, and occasionally I could spot boot prints in the dirt, showing where rangers had hiked up and down this path before us.

In the lead, Olivia continued on unwaveringly, the crayon-blue cooler bag bouncing against her back. Ellie was close behind her, and cast nervous glances at us with every few steps. Meanwhile, Zeke seemed to have installed himself as a buffer between those two and Chloe and Baylie.

At the back of the group, I struggled to hold my focus to the forest, though it kept slipping to Chloe. I hadn't had enough sleep – barely an hour, if that – and my brain felt like it had the attention span of a squirrel on speed. Try as I might, I couldn't stop my thoughts from returning to her. To the way Zeke had attempted to touch her in the kitchen, and the way she'd pulled away from him.

Almost like she'd pulled away from me yesterday.

I didn't know how to read that. I wanted to hope that was a good sign for me, that maybe she wasn't as into him as I'd thought, but that seemed like a big conclusion to jump to based on one small action that could have meant anything.

And besides, I really needed to concentrate.

Grimacing, I glanced to the trail behind us again. Winding down the hill and only partly visible between all the trees, the track seemed empty. My hearing mostly agreed, though the birds were giving me a headache and interfering with my ability to be sure.

We crested another rise and the path led down to a clearing nestled in a tiny valley, where a collection of fallen logs rested. The Park Service or time had smoothed the logs' upper sides, till they looked like natural benches for hikers. Crossing to the nearest one of these, Olivia sat down and swung the bag from her shoulder.

"Anyone hungry?" she asked, looking mostly to me and Zeke.

I shook my head, and he did the same. I hadn't eaten since we'd grabbed a meal on the road last night, but my body was too distracted by the possibility of people sneaking up on us to let my stomach worry much about food.

The others sat on the logs, with Baylie and Chloe staying near each other and leaving the rest of us to find places elsewhere.

"So I've got to say," Olivia began. "You all came at a good time. Colorado is beautiful in the summer."

I struggled to keep my irritation from my face. I wished she wouldn't try to make small talk. Between that, the birds, and my steadily growing headache, it was hard to hear if anyone was coming.

"Though," Olivia continued with a smile, "I admit I'm a bit biased. I love it when the trees are so brilliantly green."

Baylie smiled, though I could tell the expression was strained. Chloe didn't respond, her gaze on the path.

"It's great, yeah," Ellie agreed supportively.

"So where are you from, Noah?" Olivia continued. "Kansas as well?"

"California."

"Oh, that sounds nice."

I nodded, returning my attention to the trail.

A heartbeat passed, and then Olivia finally seemed to give up on her attempt at conversation.

Time crept along while the birds shrieked at each other and nothing else happened. Every few moments, my gaze twitched back to Chloe. I wondered what she was thinking about. I wondered if there was something I could do to change this situation – the one where Zeke was still in the picture. Things had just been starting to get good between us when she'd had to leave Santa Lucina because of what those dehaians had done. And yes, after that, everything had gone to hell. I'd hurt her. She'd fallen for that guy.

But there had to be a way to get the good stuff back again.

Nothing came to me. Nothing that wouldn't be stupid, anyway. Near silence – birds aside – in the middle of a group wasn't exactly the best setting for a private conversation with a girl.

I scowled, fighting the urge to rub at my burning eyes for the twentieth time. My family and that Harman guy just wouldn't give us a break. Whenever I turned around, they seemed to be after us again.

A buzzing noise made me tense. I glanced over to see Ellie pulling out her cell phone. Her brow furrowed when she read the caller ID and then she tucked it away again.

"Who was it?" Baylie asked, her quiet voice seeming loud after everyone's silence.

"I don't know. I didn't recognize the number."

I returned to watching the forest.

A minute passed. The buzzing came again.

Ellie drew out the phone. "It's the same number. Should I answer it?"

"Probably just someone convinced they're not wrong about what they dialed," Baylie replied. "They'll give up in a minute."

Ellie nodded, though she still appeared concerned.

My gaze snapped over as the thud of footsteps came from farther back along the trail. My brow drew down. My cousins wouldn't be that loud. Harman might, but that sounded like at least three people.

I turned back to find Chloe watching me. I glanced to

Olivia, but the woman was studying the other direction of the path.

I gave Chloe a quick nod.

She shifted anxiously on the log.

"Hello?" a man called.

Olivia turned. "Over here, Phil."

I rose to my feet, listening for anyone else around us, and from the corner of my eye, I saw the others stand as well.

Breathing heavily, a large, middle-aged man strode up to the crest of the hill. Sweat shone on his face and balding head, and the red flush of his skin probably owed as much to the polyester sports jacket he wore despite the summer's heat as it did to the hike. Two others followed him, one of them a petite woman with long and gray-streaked brown hair who was dressed like she'd just been dropped out of a time-warp from Woodstock, and the second was a blond guy in a striped polo shirt who looked as if he belonged in some high-end suburban neighborhood, where he'd most likely be obsessing over his lawn.

"So!" the first man announced while he came down the slope toward us. "Quite the secret meeting you've got going, Olivia. You sure we had to come all the way out here for this?"

"Of course she is, Phil," the Woodstock woman replied. "Like I said back by the cars, Olivia wouldn't ask us here without a good reason."

The suburban guy gave a quick nod of agreement, though he kept an eye to Phil as if concerned the man would see the motion.

"And besides," the woman continued. She drew a deep breath of the forest air. "This is a *much* nicer place to meet. No offense to your office," she added to Olivia.

"None taken." Olivia glanced to us. "Everyone, I'd like you to meet the elders of the landwalkers. A few of them, anyway. Dave, Phil," she nodded to the two men, "and Robin."

"Hello," Robin said with a smile.

"Hi," Phil offered shortly, his attention more on tugging a handkerchief from his sports jacket than on us. "So what's the big secret, Olivia?" He swiped the sweat off his bald head. "It's hotter than hell out here. Why'd we have to–"

"If you would allow me to explain," Olivia interrupted evenly. "I asked you out here because something has occurred that requires our attention and our assistance. This is Chloe. She is half-landwalker, half-dehaian. And she survived the change."

Phil froze halfway through stuffing the kerchief back into his pocket.

Robin's brown eyes widened. "She–"

"Are you *sure*?" Phil demanded. He turned to Chloe. "Young lady, you can't just make claims like that and expect no one to–"

"I've seen proof." Olivia looked to Chloe, raising an eyebrow. "If you'd please?"

Chloe hesitated. I couldn't blame her. Robin seemed like a kid with a new toy, while Phil just appeared ready to bulldoze over everyone here on his way back to the car. Dave stood behind them both, his eyes on Chloe like he couldn't decide whether to retreat.

With a quick glance to Baylie, Chloe let her spikes emerge from her forearms.

Robin's mouth dropped open and Dave gave in, moving back a step like he'd obviously wanted to do. Phil's gaze snapped from Chloe's arms to her face, as though he couldn't figure out how the two were attached to the same person.

I barely kept myself from getting up to make them stop staring. I hated it when people did that, mostly because I knew how much Chloe hated it too.

It didn't help that it'd happened so often in the past few days.

But she wasn't a freak. Or some kind of landwalker savior thing. I wished people would quit treating her like she was.

"Unfortunately, we are not the first to find out about Chloe," Olivia continued. "Her parents, who had previously not heard of the treatments now available to half-dehaian children, sought the assistance of Harman Brooks in repressing those traits *after* she survived changing." She paused. "I'm given to understand it did not go well. But with the help of my student and Chloe's friends, she was able to escape and recover."

The others glanced to the girls. Ellie dropped her gaze to the forest floor, visibly embarrassed at their attention.

"Harman also got his hands on another person," Olivia said. "Someone who, by all rights, shouldn't be here."

She glanced over. "This is Zeke. He's a full-blood dehaian."

The expressions of surprise had been fading from the others' faces, but now they came back in full force.

"Are you s–" Phil began.

"Oh, for heaven's sake, don't start that again," Robin interrupted. She looked to Chloe. "He is?"

Chloe blinked uncomfortably. "Um, yeah?"

Robin nodded as if that was all she needed to hear. "And how is he here?"

"Her," Olivia said when Chloe paused.

They returned to their staring. My jaw clenching, I fought the urge to order them to stop.

"You all know the stories," Olivia continued. "What it means for a person like Chloe to exist. There have already been signs that the creature of legend is returning – the storms on the coast, the seismic readings from the seafloor. And that is why I've called you together. Harman doesn't believe in this. You know that; I know that. But given what he has *already* tried to do to her, if he got his hands on Chloe again, there is no question that he would continue experimenting on her. Meanwhile, her parents will also insist upon exposing her to the treatments again. We can't let that happen. Repressing what she is won't resolve this – though I realize that wasn't her parents' intent – and experimenting upon her is intolerable. So we need to keep Chloe protected and stop what's happening at the same time." She paused. "And I'm open to suggestions."

The three of them stood there, staring like idiots and doing nothing useful.

"What have you ruled out so far?" Robin asked.

"Nothing. This is the first we're discussing it."

Robin frowned. "Okay…"

"Why not simply mask the magic coming off of her?" Phil suggested like we were all stupid for not thinking of it.

"How?" Robin asked.

"Put her underground."

My eyebrows rose and I saw Zeke's do the same. Incredulous, Baylie sat up straighter, looking ready to interpose herself between Chloe and anyone who thought to make good on that idea.

Dave cleared his throat. "What about–"

"The original dehaians tried that," Robin interrupted, shaking her head. "They lived underground for fifteen years and it didn't work. In the Vlostine account, there's clear evidence they even–"

Phil made a rude noise. "I've read Vlostine. He was a moron. He wanted them to wear wire-rimmed skullcaps, for pity's sake. But if you examine Dartinian's records, they show that–"

"Oh, come on!" Robin countered. "Dartinian was a hack who couldn't even *read*! He needed scribes to write down his theories, and he couldn't tell if they got the words right!" She scoffed. "Underground. Honestly, Phil. If we go by the information from the archives of Longtiel, it shows that the original dehaians knew–"

Phil gave a bark of laughter. "Longtiel? You must be joking. How many times have I told you, Longtiel wasn't even considered reputable in his own–"

"And *Dartinian* was?" Robin retorted.

The throbbing in my head worsened. Seated on the logs, the others looked like they were developing headaches of their own, while behind Robin and Phil, Dave kept clearing his throat and attempting to speak, though he never succeeded in getting a word in edgewise.

"Dartinian recorded thousands of dehaians living on land at that point in history," Phil argued. "This is just one girl. The difference in scale makes this a viable strategy."

"We could try–" Dave started.

"Scale is irrelevant!" Robin cried.

I looked away. They wouldn't stick Chloe in a hole in the ground. I'd make sure they'd regret it if they tried.

And meanwhile, I wished they'd keep it down. The idiots could probably be heard for miles.

Taking a deep breath, I closed my eyes, trying to concentrate on the sounds of the forest beyond their arguing.

Birds shrieked. There was a river not too far to our left.

"We have new technologies now," Phil snapped. "We could shield her location in ways those dehaians couldn't even have dreamed."

"Technology isn't the issue," Robin replied. "Magic is energy. It will permeate the–"

"Energy frequencies can be disrupted," he retorted.

I grimaced, struggling to hear anything past their voices.

A rustling came from deeper in the forest to my right. A branch snapped, and then another. More leaves rustled.

I opened my eyes, looking toward the noise.

"You can't be serious," Robin snapped.

"Says the woman suggesting we use Longtiel as a reference."

I fought to focus. Something was coming this way. Maybe someone.

It could just be a bear.

That didn't make me feel better.

The rustling sound came again, closer this time. A voice murmured, the words too low and distant for even my ears to pick them out.

My heart began to pound harder. Someone *was* coming. Someone avoiding the main path.

That couldn't be good.

I hesitated. I needed a way to tell the others without those idiot landwalker elders learning what I was. Chloe hadn't said anything about that to Olivia and from what I could tell, Ellie hadn't either – though God knew why. But I appreciated it.

If I had it my way, the fewer people who knew I wasn't human, the better.

I glanced to Chloe. She was looking back and forth between Phil and Robin like she was watching the tennis match from hell. At her side, Baylie held one hand protectively to Chloe's arm, while Ellie was studying her phone, which was once again buzzing.

I swallowed, scanning the clearing. There had to be a way to get their attention.

Zeke was watching me.

I hesitated, but there wasn't another option. The girls weren't looking our way.

My gaze twitched illustratively back toward the forest. He drew a breath, tensing.

At Chloe's side, Baylie caught sight of his motion. She looked to me and obviously read something of what was going on from my face.

"Uh, guys?" she called.

"And I don't believe we can just– what?" Robin cut off.

"I, um… I think someone's coming," Baylie finished.

They all paused. Olivia's eyebrow climbed.

"*Excuse* me?" Phil asked, disbelief clear in his voice. Craning his neck, he looked beyond us to the trail, while Robin leaned past him to do the same.

Dave fidgeted anxiously. "Were you expecting anyone else?"

Olivia shook her head, still studying Baylie.

I took the opportunity to move closer to the trees, straining to hear anything more. I couldn't pick up on any of my cousins, although that didn't mean much. Stupid as they were, they'd still know I'd be near Chloe. They'd hide their presences so I wouldn't be able to tell they were coming.

Though, on that account, they also wouldn't make noise. Or talk. They were good enough hunters to be careful about that, especially when they knew I'd hear them.

My brow drew down. Something wasn't right.

A rustle came from beyond the opposite side of the clearing.

I looked back toward the sound.

"We need to go," Baylie said, seeing my expression. "Now."

Chloe and Zeke were already getting to their feet.

Another branch snapped, the sound coming from a different direction entirely.

A breath left my chest. We were surrounded.

How the hell had anyone gotten around us without me hearing them?

I pushed the thought aside. The answer was standing in the middle of the clearing, still seeming like they wanted to continue their argument. And meanwhile, I was burning time.

I strode toward Chloe and Baylie.

Ellie looked between us and Olivia. "What do we do?"

Olivia just watched us, saying nothing.

Something inside me went cold. She wasn't helping. She only stood there.

Like we were a science experiment. Like she'd set this up.

"Come on," I said, jerking my head toward the far side of the clearing. I hadn't heard anyone that way yet. Maybe they hadn't gotten that far.

Chloe nodded and hurried after me, with Baylie and Ellie sticking close behind. When I reached the next rise, I glanced back to see Zeke throwing a quick look to the other directions and then following as well.

"Now hang on," Phil blustered, starting after us. "We don't have any evidence there's anyone actually–"

"Excuse me, folks."

I froze. I knew that voice.

Turning, I looked back at the camp. A portly man wearing

a brown police uniform walked out of the forest. Two guys followed him, both dressed in camouflage with rifles strapped to their backs, and I didn't recognize them at all. But the portly guy was the police chief from Reidsburg. The one Chloe had been anxious about, back that day when her parents had taken her to the station.

Right before they'd heard about Harman. Right before they'd brought her to Iowa to be experimented upon.

It was hard to keep my skin from changing.

Two other men walked through the underbrush on either side of the clearing, one of them that nervous police officer from Reidsburg – Aaron or Adam or something – and the other a guy in camo gear who was damn near twice the scrawny cop's size.

I tensed, putting my money on the last guy being greliaran if any of them were.

A branch snapped behind me. Another man with a rifle stepped from the forest onto the path.

"What seems to be the trouble, officer?" Olivia asked carefully, her dark eyes scanning the people surrounding us.

"Well, ma'am, my friends and I were looking for a group of runaways, and we had reason to believe you'd know where to find them. Local park ranger told us you might be up here and—" Chloe stopped breathing when he glanced to her. "—seems we were right. So now I'd like to ask you to turn those kids over to us. I'd hate for this to get awkward."

"I don't know anything about any runaways, officer," Olivia

answered. "These are my business associates and our children. We were just having a picnic."

She gestured to the blue cooler bag and then glanced to the other three elders, something sharp in her eyes.

The chief gave her a weary look. "Ma'am, I imagine you know me and my friends here pretty well, just like we know you and your 'business associates'. Doctor Brooks sent us, so I'd appreciate it if you'd drop the act. These kids are runaways. One of them's got her grandfather back in town, worried sick and hoping she's safe. And one of them's going to be taken in for murder in not too much longer, once we settle the question of how he's here." His gaze flicked to Zeke and then returned to Olivia. "So with all due respect, please get out of our way."

Olivia paused. "If you know who we are, then you realize how bad an idea it is to argue with us."

The men surrounding us tensed. Fear in her eyes, Ellie glanced back to us and then retreated up the trail, coming closer to Chloe and me.

My brow drew down warily.

"But we're trying to help Chloe," protested the scrawny cop on the far side of the clearing. "Surely you can see that? Just help. You don't need to—"

"Quiet, Aaron," the chief ordered, not taking his eyes from Olivia. "Yes, ma'am," he acknowledged carefully. "I do know. But I hope *you* realize that we're here with the backing of your *other* business associates. And they want these kids to come home too."

"T-they wouldn't agree to this," Dave stammered.

The chief rested his hand on the gun attached to his belt, his expression unchanged. "They have."

No one moved. I made myself keep breathing.

"Alright," Robin said.

I looked to the petite woman in alarm.

She stepped past Olivia, holding out her hands peaceably. "Alright. Just take it easy. There's no need for this. Just look around. No one wants to see bad things happen in so nice a place. If everyone's decided to make this problem disappear, then we need to go along with that." Robin looked back. "Right? I'm sure everyone knows how important it is for us to stick together on these things."

Dave gave a jerky nod, while Phil simply grunted with annoyance and turned a tired glare on the scrawny cop and his behemoth companion.

Olivia didn't move. "You'll regret this, Robin."

The woman smiled as if the idea amused her. "I doubt it. You heard him. Everyone else is in agreement and I'd rather not go rogue, if it's all the same to you. I like my job."

Olivia's jaw tightened. She looked away, finding the man standing behind us, and after a heartbeat, she sighed.

I stared at them. I couldn't believe this was happening.

"Okay, then." Robin turned to the police chief with a smile. "Go on."

In unison, the landwalker elders closed their eyes and darted in different directions like kids playing both roles in a game of hide-and-seek simultaneously.

The guys around the clearing shouted in alarm.

I stared at the elders in confusion, and then my gaze snapped to the cop and his friends.

The men were blinking or squinting at the forest. Their hands went to their faces and then flung outward, swiping at the air in front of them.

As though they were blind.

Footsteps charged us. I spun and then stumbled back when the man on the trail behind us ran forward, his hands clutching at the air as if to grab anything in reach.

Chloe and the others scattered. The man staggered past them, moving like he was dizzy or drunk, and then a root caught his foot, sending him sprawling to the ground.

We stared. Gasping, he fumbled at the rocks and branches as though he couldn't figure out what they were. With a furious cry, he shoved away from the ground, trying unsteadily to reach his feet.

Ellie turned to us. "Go," she mouthed desperately.

I looked from her to the chaos in the clearing, and then I snagged Chloe's arm. Pulling her with me, I took off down the trail.

CHLOE

With frantic glances over my shoulder, I ran after Noah along the path. His hand held my arm like a vice and he was moving so fast, Baylie and Ellie were having trouble keeping up. Behind them, Zeke followed with an eye to the trail, his every motion ready for a fight even if he hadn't let any spikes come out yet.

I couldn't blame him. Harman had sent Chief Reynolds after us, along with the chief's nephew and a bunch of guys who looked like they belonged on a hunting reality show.

And meanwhile, the landwalker elders had superpowers.

I swallowed hard. Landwalkers didn't have magic. That was sort of their thing. They were basically human, just with an allergy to the ocean and a really weird history. That was it.

And Mom and Dad couldn't do that. They couldn't do anything like that at all.

They *absolutely* would have used it on me otherwise.

A gunshot rang out behind us. I stumbled to a stop and

looked back.

The forest was still and we were fine. But it sounded like someone in the clearing had gotten their hands on their gun.

"Come on," Noah said, his voice tight.

We kept running. The trail dipped briefly and then rose again to climb higher along the mountainside. Past the dense tree cover, more mountains surrounded us, all of them appearing impossibly close. In the valley below, a river flowed like a ribbon of silver and blue. The sunlight hit us in fuller force when we continued out of the shadow of the slopes, bringing the summer heat with it.

I had no idea where we were going.

Noah seemed to have the same thought. Casting a quick look over his shoulder to the trail, he slowed. "Where to?" he asked Ellie.

The girl choked down a breath. "Mom and Dad live a few miles from–"

"Harman could be there," Zeke cut in.

Breathing hard, Ellie hesitated. "We could hide. Olivia and the others will find us."

"Or Chief Reynolds could," Baylie countered.

Ellie's desperate expression grew stronger. "I don't know what else to do."

Noah frowned, glancing to the trail again.

"We keep going," Zeke said. "Circle back to the car and get out of here."

I looked between him and Noah. Of all of us, they had to

be the most exhausted, and the car was miles from here.

"The trail doesn't connect," Ellie said, almost as if apologizing for the path. "It… it just goes on to join up with others deeper into the mountains. You have to go back the way you came to reach the parking lot."

I let out a breath. "Then yeah, we need to hide. Wait for those elders to find us and tell us if the coast is clear."

Grimaces crossed the others' faces, all of them tinged by varying degrees of fatigue or concern. Baylie hadn't been wrong either. Chief Reynolds or his goons could find us instead. But then, they'd probably have split up by now, so maybe we'd only have to deal with one or two of them.

And that was doable. *Terrifying*… but doable.

My stomach churned.

"Is there any place safe around here?" Zeke asked.

Ellie thought for a second. "Well, the Midnight Cave isn't too far. We could hide there."

"Somewhere less obvious?" Baylie prompted. "The trail's named for that. It's probably the first place they'll try to find us."

Ellie looked helpless. "I-I don't know anywhere else close. I mean–"

"Fine," I cut in. "Which way?"

"I think…" Ellie checked around as if trying to get her bearings. "Up through here will be fastest."

Still giving anxious glances to the direction of the gunshot, she started up the overgrown slope to the left of the trail.

We followed.

Brambles scratched my legs and caught on my shoes. Ellie murmured occasionally, pointing out poisonous plants or other hazards with her voice so low, I needed to strain to hear her. There wasn't a path to speak of. There wasn't anything, and when I looked back, I could barely trace our trail through the brush.

Which was a good thing, really. I just hoped we could find our way out of here if we had to keep moving after the cave.

We crested the rise. Ellie continued on, leading us around the slope and then down another, and every branch and dried leaf that cracked under our feet sounded like a gunshot in the quiet.

"There," she said, pointing.

A strange contortion of the landscape had conspired to create a dip in the mountainside, as though a giant had taken a scoop to the slope and carved out a space. Shadows hung thick within the hollow, while a black space at the base marked the opening to the cave. Vines and tree roots dangled from the top of the thirty-foot-high entrance, though the sides were clear. When we came closer, I could see that amateur graffiti artists had taken advantage of that latter fact, opting to leave scribbles of their names along the boulders' smooth faces. Grit dusted the cave floor, with a few cigarette butts tossed there as well. Beside the entrance, signs stood watch, warning everyone that flashlights and caution were needed for the area.

We hurried inside, and the air of the cave made the sweat

on my skin cool instantly. The massive space was like a refrigerator, and the darkness was absolute.

I looked back. A narrow track ran up to the entrance. Sunlight shone down on it, though the brightness ended a few yards shy of the cave opening as a result of the strange shape of the mountainside.

"I'll stay out of sight close to the entrance," Noah said quietly. "Signal if I hear anyone coming."

I glanced over and caught him watching me. I hesitated.

His brow twitched up, insistent.

I swallowed hard. "Okay."

"Go ahead and do what you need to do to get deeper in there," he continued. "Just don't look toward the front till you've changed them back. If anyone comes this way, they might be able to spot the glow in the darkness."

Drawing a breath, I nodded.

"Another dehaian thing," Noah explained, glancing to Baylie. "Don't freak out."

She paused. "Alright…"

I let my eyes change. The darkness vanished, becoming nothing more than faint shadows and revealing a massive cavern that stretched back for hundreds of feet till a metal gate installed by the Park Service barred access to the area beyond. Water and time had worn dips and holes into the uneven cave floor, though someone had taken care to spray-paint rings around the worst of the depressions as a warning. Bulky protrusions of rock warped the cavern walls, most of them worn smooth by the same forces that had pocked the floor. Moisture dripped from the distant ceiling, staining the stone in mold-encrusted swaths.

Baylie's breath caught when I looked over at her. Beside her, Zeke watched me, his eyes glowing brilliant sapphire blue.

"What–" Baylie started, and then she blinked. "Seeing in the dark. Olivia said–"

"Just stick close to us," I cut in. "Okay?"

She nodded, still staring at me.

I took her hand and then glanced to Zeke. He extended a hand to Ellie. The girl hesitated, nervousness written across her face stronger than ever, but after a heartbeat, she gingerly placed her fingers on his.

We started into the cave.

"Careful," I whispered to Baylie when we neared a dip in the floor. Even to my eyes, the hole was dark, and I could hear water trickling down from it into whatever lay beyond. A grate covered the opening, the metal bars drilled straight into the rock. "Just a bit left… yeah."

Her shoes scraped on the dirt and gravel.

"And left again, a little more…" I continued as we passed another hole.

Ellie squeaked with fright behind me and I fought the urge to look back to check on her. The glaring sunlight outside the cave would probably hurt if I looked directly toward it, given how adjusted to the dark my eyes were right now.

"You're okay," I heard Zeke whisper.

A choked sound answered his words, like Ellie was trying not to cry.

I kept going, maneuvering across the pockmarked floor. I could hear Baylie breathing beside me, the sound short and tense, and her hand trembled in mine.

"Around that rock there, Chloe," Zeke murmured.

I nodded, seeing what he was suggesting. About ten yards ahead of the Park Service's gate at the rear of the cave, a bulbous mass of stone stuck out from the wall. Larger than all the rest, the protrusion was nearly the height of the cavern itself. We'd be utterly invisible behind it.

"Little bit farther," I told Baylie. "There's a rock up here. We're going to get behind it."

She made a noise of agreement.

I led her around the side of the rock. Nothing much waited there; just moist gravel and mold that made my nose itch. Reaching up with my free hand, I gripped her shoulder and Baylie's breath caught again.

"It's kind of slimy back here," I whispered. "Just stay put. You're fine right where you are."

Baylie nodded. Her gaze darted across the black, focusing on nothing, and then returned to me.

"This is weird," she told me softly.

"Yeah," I agreed.

I squeezed her hand and then glanced to Zeke. One hand on Ellie's shoulder and the other crushed in her trembling grip, he guided her to a stop behind the boulder. The girl's eyes were closed and I could see her chest rising and falling in rapid gasps.

"You alright, Ellie?" I asked.

Her head moved in a jerky motion, as if she was forcing herself to nod even though she wanted to shake her head. "I-I hate the dark. I always just… if we could be like you guys… wouldn't be so bad…"

Zeke's mouth tightened. "You're fine. Just keep breathing."

The nod-shake motion came again.

I looked in the direction of the entrance, though the huge rock obstructed my view. Noah could probably hear us, but hopefully no one else could.

Though if Chief Reynolds had brought greliarans with him…

I swallowed hard.

"What was that back there, Ellie?" I whispered. "The elders?"

The furrows in her brow deepened. "I, um…"

"Just *tell* us," Baylie snapped, her quiet voice tense.

I glanced to her, seeing the stress she was trying to hide flash across her face. My hand squeezed hers again. She took a breath, the expression fading.

"Sorry," Baylie whispered.

An anxious smile of acknowledgement flitted across Ellie's face.

"I thought landwalkers didn't have magic," I said.

"We don't. At least, Olivia never called it that…"

Ellie's face crumpled. She bit her lip to stop it from trembling.

I paused. "I'm sure they're fine. Noah would have told us if it'd sounded like someone got hurt."

Her expression cleared a bit and she nodded, accepting the words even though I was fairly certain they were a lie.

Noah would protect us from that, just like he was doing right now.

My gaze flicked to the boulder blocking my view of the cave front. It took effort to pull it back again.

"It's not magic," Ellie started, her quiet voice determined. "It's like… you know that thing dehaians do? The make-people-love-you thing?"

"Aveluria," Zeke said.

Ellie nodded. "Yeah. But they say it used to be more… complicated. Not just like those old siren myths, where mermaids lured sailors to their deaths, but more like those stories where the mermaids kissed sailors and took them down into the ocean. But the sailors didn't die. Or, at least, not all the time.

"Some records claim the dehaians used to be able to do that. And when they split, becoming like him–" she nodded in Zeke's general direction, "–and us, that magic thing split too. But it's not easy for us like it is for dehaians, especially not anymore. Most landwalkers can't do it. Can't even hope to. And even if you *do* have the talent for it, it still takes years to master the ability; that's why learning to be an elder takes so long. They're the only ones with the discipline and training to use that skill. And it isn't really like the dehaians' thing, anyway. Avah… what you called it."

My brow furrowed. "But what *can* you do?"

"It's more of a mental thing. It's not exactly magic."

"Looked pretty magical to me," Baylie muttered.

Ellie grimaced. "It's just… it's like projection. Sort of. The elder can make people be like them, in a way. Like back there. The elders all closed their eyes, kind of making themselves blind, and then the men they'd locked onto were blind as well. The elders ran, disorienting themselves, and the guys were disoriented too. It's not like telepathy or mind-reading. It's like… the ability to basically *project* onto that other person a… a way of being."

"Can *you* do that?" Baylie asked warily.

Ellie looked down. "I-I'm training, but I haven't yet. Grandpa's a master. Olivia is too. Robin, all of them. I know a bit of how they talk about it, the codes and stuff. That's what Robin was doing back there: telling the others what to do about the guys surrounding us. I know that, but when it comes to the rest, I'm… I'm just not that talented."

I hesitated, and I could see Baylie and Zeke do the same.

"So if your grandfather could do that, why didn't he try it on me?" Zeke asked after a moment, disgust tingeing his tone. "Get answers to his questions that way?"

"It doesn't work like that," Ellie said. "It just makes people the same as the elder, like, in what that elder is experiencing. Or makes the elder like them, though that's a whole lot harder. But back when it used to work for the original dehaians, we think it let them bring people with them. Underwater, I mean.

Make people able to be the same as them in that way. Go where they could. But that was it."

I froze, and then my gaze snapped to Zeke.

He was looking at me too.

"A-and how did that work?" I asked without taking my eyes from him. "Did it, like, ever wear off?"

"Wear off?" Ellie repeated, sounding confused. "I don't think…"

She went quiet. I glanced over to find her looking between us.

"I'm such a *moron*," she whispered. "You brought–"

"Yeah," I replied softly.

She swallowed hard. "I don't think it did. From everything Olivia's told me, it sounded like as long as someone was alive to keep the magic going, it'd never change."

"Did their distance from each other matter?" I pressed.

Ellie shrugged in the darkness. "I don't think so."

I let out the breath I hadn't realized I'd been holding. That was about the best news I'd heard lately. I'd been so worried about Zeke when Harman had taken him, and to know that whatever I'd done wouldn't suddenly disappear, or that being apart from him wouldn't leave him dead… relief wasn't even the half of it.

I looked over to find him studying the ground, his face tight. My brow furrowed in confusion, the relief evaporating.

Gravel clattered on the cave floor behind us, interrupting me before I could ask him what was wrong. As a group, we turned toward the sound.

Seconds slid by. Voices carried down the length of the cave.

Baylie's grip tightened on my hand. Warped and distorted, the voices were hard to understand, but none of them sounded like Noah.

"Hello?" a man called, his voice bouncing off the cave walls.

A moment passed. The man murmured something as though speaking to another person and over the distance, I couldn't make sense of his words.

Baylie's fingers were crushing mine.

A flashlight beam pierced the darkness and swept over the cave. I winced, the light burning before I could change my eyes enough to compensate.

"Hey," the man said. "Come out of there."

I stopped breathing. They'd found Noah.

"Where are your friends?"

Noah's response was too low to hear.

The man chuckled. "Nice try, kid. They back there?"

Footsteps headed toward us, and the beam of the flashlight came with them.

I looked to Zeke.

The glow of his eyes vanished only a heartbeat slower than mine.

Even with the flashlights coming toward us, the darkness was incredible.

The beams swung around the boulder. I squinted and ducked my face away, the lights burning all over again.

Two men who looked like weightlifters in camo paused when they spotted us. Shotguns hung on their shoulders and sheathed knives were strapped to their waists. Full-sleeve tattoos covered the arms of one of them, while the other had a vicious scar down the side of his face.

"Found them," the tattooed one called back to the front of the cave. The flashlight beam swept across us. "The Kowalski girl and the granddaughter are here too."

Without waiting for a response, the scarred one moved into the beam of light, reaching to grab my arm.

Zeke stepped in front of me.

The man paused. His head turned back toward his companion, though his gaze didn't leave Zeke. "He the–"

"Yeah."

The man's hand moved so fast. In an eye-blink, he had the knife drawn and pointed at Zeke. "You just stay–"

A snarl came from the front of the cave. A scream followed, the sound cutting short a moment later with a thud. The men with the flashlights spun as pounding footsteps raced toward us.

Their eyes went wide.

"Get the girls!" the tattooed guy yelled, dropping his flashlight and scrambling to yank his gun around.

The other guy came at us, the knife still gripped in his fist. He grabbed Zeke, trying to shove him out of the way.

A wall slammed into the tattooed man, throwing him hard into the barred gate at the rear of the cave. The scarred guy looked toward his companion, his face aghast, and then he spun, stabbing at Zeke.

Spikes rushed from Zeke's forearms. He stepped back, avoiding the blade, and then swung at the man. The guy twisted, the spikes tearing through his shirt and grazing his skin in bloodied lines.

Hands grabbed the man from behind, yanked him backward, and sent him into the barred gate after the tattooed guy.

Noah watched them for a heartbeat and then looked to us, the glowing fissures on his face closing.

"Everyone alright?" His gaze scanned over us hurriedly. "I saw the guy going for a knife…"

"Yeah," Zeke replied, his spikes already gone. "Fine."

Noah glanced to me, his brow twitching up for confirmation.

I gave a tight nod.

He exhaled and then bent quickly, retrieving the flashlight the man had dropped. "We should get out of here. They could have friends in the area."

Baylie moved past me, coming near her stepbrother. Ellie followed.

My gaze slipped to Zeke. He didn't look over as he motioned for me to go after them.

I hesitated and then did as he asked, following the others silently from the hollow behind the boulder.

Gravel crunching under our feet, we trailed the brilliant beam of the flashlight back the way we had come a few minutes before. Beyond the bright opening of the cave, the path appeared empty and shadowed beneath the dense tree cover.

I resisted the urge to let my gaze go to Zeke while I walked. I'd seen his arms. The spikes, when they came out of his skin. They weren't all there. Like gaps in the tines of a broken-toothed comb, only a random few of the blades remained.

And I didn't know what to say. Maybe they'd grow back. Maybe it didn't hurt to have them removed – though I doubted it. The mere thought made my skin crawl. But maybe…

I swallowed, my stomach twisting. Maybe nothing. Harman was a monster.

We reached the entrance. A man lay crumpled against the wall, though his chest moved to show he was still alive. Noah's jaw tightened when Baylie glanced to him, her brow rising. Without meeting her gaze, he thumbed off the switch on the flashlight and headed for the path outside.

And then he froze. Turning with a look on his face like he wanted to swear, he motioned for us to go back.

We hurried into the shelter of the cave again.

"That way," Noah whispered, pointing to the right. "Maybe two people."

"Head over there," Zeke told me. "Stay as low as you can."

Noah handed Baylie the flashlight. Quickly, she and Ellie retreated to a small cluster of boulders near the wall and ducked down behind it.

"Chloe?" Zeke pressed.

I trailed Baylie, glancing back to the guys while I went.

"Come on," Zeke said to Noah. He strode toward the cave entrance.

Noah's face tightened, but after a heartbeat's hesitation, he followed.

I crouched beside Baylie, attempting to stay out of sight behind the too-small boulder. Bracing my hands on the side of the stone for balance, I strained to hear any indications of trouble from the entrance.

Minutes crept past. No sound came from the cave opening, and only birds called in the forest beyond. My brow drew down. How far away had these people been when Noah picked up on them?

Greliaran hearing was incredible.

Footsteps crunched on gravel. At my side, Baylie's breath caught.

"Hello?" a man called warily, like he was almost afraid of actually being heard.

A heartbeat passed. I heard more scraping of gravel.

"You're here," the man said. "Are the others—"

"Chloe?" Olivia called. "Ellie?"

Ellie scrambled up from behind the rock.

Moving more slowly, I rose with Baylie, cautiously eyeing the cave entrance.

Olivia and Dave stood there. A few yards away from the two elders, and from each other, Zeke and Noah watched them while casting quick looks to the forest in case anyone else followed.

"Are you alright?" Ellie cried, hurrying toward Olivia.

"Fine," Olivia replied.

"What happened?" the girl pressed. "Where are the others? We heard a gunshot."

Olivia's lips thinned as if she didn't really want to talk about it. "Mr. Reynolds got his hands on his weapon. He tried shooting at us to break the connection, but thankfully he missed." She paused. "Barely." Her jaw worked briefly, as though she was fighting the urge to add more colorful words to the story. "Right now, Phil and Robin are heading in the opposite direction from us, and hopefully leading the rest of those men on a wild goose chase at the same time."

She skimmed her gaze over us, landing at last on me. "Are you all okay?"

I glanced to Baylie and then nodded.

"Good," Olivia said. "Then we need to get out of here. You all have your car back at the parking lot. Take it and follow us. We have a plan to reduce the Beast's ability to draw strength from what you are."

I hesitated. "What plan?"

"We can talk once we get there."

I barely kept myself from scoffing. That comment sounded so like my parents, it was absurd.

"No," I said, shaking my head. "No, you tell us now. What plan?"

Olivia's mouth tightened again. "There's an old mine about thirty miles from here. You can stay there for a while. We need to mask that signal coming off of you. I understand the arguments against it, but right now, putting you underground is our best choice till we can figure this out."

I stared at her while Baylie and the others voiced protests around me.

"No," I stated emphatically. "No, there's no *way* I'm doing that."

"Chloe, we don't have a better option."

"What about the original dehaians' solution?" Dave offered.

Olivia turned to him. "What?"

"I wanted to say back there... what about the *actual* solution? What they did?"

She stared at him, incredulous. "We don't have the ability to do that."

"No, but–"

"Dave, we can't do that," Olivia insisted. "We're just going to have to–"

"Joseph can," Dave finished in a rush over her words.

Olivia stopped. My brow drew down.

"Joseph." Olivia's voice was flat and her expression was the same. "Joseph is a terrible idea."

Dave shifted his weight uncomfortably. "But he could. And it worked for them."

"What... what solution?" I asked, my stomach fluttering.

"Splitting themselves," Olivia explained without looking

away from Dave. "Taking away one side of their abilities."

"That almost *killed* Chloe!" Baylie cried. "You can't try that!"

Dave shook his head. "This wouldn't be like what Harman attempted. It's not drugs and treatments for the rest of her life; it'd be permanent. Magic-based. It'd change what she is completely. And if anyone can do that, it's Joseph." He paused, watching Olivia. "The Vlostine account is right. Underground won't work. And even if it did, you can't keep the girl in a bunker for the rest of her life."

Olivia looked like she might've considered trying.

"Who's Joseph?" I asked hurriedly.

Dave hesitated. "You might find it a bit hard to believe…"

"Or you might not." Olivia's gaze went to Baylie. "You're one of them, aren't you? A greliaran."

Baylie's eyebrows shot up. "What? I'm not–"

"You heard the men coming. You said it yourself, and since no one else heard a thing, it was clearly a greliaran ability that enabled you to do so. You also knew about the deal between landwalkers and greliarans. And your anger when I called your kind monsters… that was telling."

Speechless, Baylie floundered.

"Hey," Noah protested, moving protectively to his stepsister's side. "Come on, she–" He faltered for a heartbeat. "Greliarans don't look like she does."

Olivia gave Noah a sympathetic glance. "Appearances can be deceiving, and the other evidence is there. Ellie told me you two aren't related by blood, so you wouldn't share those traits. And greliarans are notoriously secretive about what they are. It's one of the first things greliaran parents teach their children. I'm sorry; it makes sense that you wouldn't have known." She looked from me to Baylie. "How you managed to be friends with a dehaian, though… I'd love an answer to that."

"I'm not greliaran," Baylie insisted, shaking her head. "We just know about them because of what Harman did. And the forest… it was just luck that I–"

"Enough," Noah snapped when Olivia's expression took on a dry cast. "She's not greliaran. I–"

"Exactly," I cut in.

Noah glanced to me.

I kept my focus on Olivia, my heart pounding. "Alright? I've known her even longer than Noah. She's not. So who's Joseph?" I looked between her and Dave when they didn't respond. "*Huh?*"

"He made the greliarans," Dave answered.

I froze.

"What?" Noah said softly.

Dave let out a breath, visibly uncomfortable with being the center of attention. "He made them. The greliarans, back in the war when the Beast was created. Joseph was on the other side; a 'wizard'… or, you know, a human who'd figured out how to use magic. The dehaians won the war, though, and most of the wizards were killed. Maybe all of them except him, since Joseph's the only one we've ever met. And he didn't want to die. He'd seen so much death. He had this ability to control magic, however, and he…"

"He used it," Olivia filled in. "He made himself immortal. Sort of."

My brow drew down. "Sort of?"

I glanced to Noah. I wasn't even sure he was breathing.

"You'd understand if you saw him."

"When," Dave amended. He grimaced. "Olivia, if *anyone* can do what the originals did–"

"Won't he just try to kill her?" Noah interjected, his voice a bit unsteady. "Finish that war? If this is the guy who made greliarans, then–"

"This is our best option," Dave said. "The Beast *will* draw on your friend. I-I've studied this. The old stories. What we used to be. Even if we don't know everything of what that creature is capable of, I'm still sure of that part." He looked to me. "Chances are, the Beast will get stronger, even with you here. The storms on the coast and the earthquakes under the ocean show it already has. And the stronger it gets, the more it'll be able to feed on what you are." He swallowed. "That thing absorbs magic. Takes magic and makes it a part of itself. And it does that as easily as we can breathe. The longer this goes on, the weaker you'll become, regardless of where you try to hide."

I stared at him. "I feel fine. I'm not–"

"That will probably change as the Beast grows more power-ful," Dave insisted. "I'm sorry. Even if you *could* somehow suppress the signal coming from you, it wouldn't matter. Some of the oldest accounts talk about the dehaians trying that. Apparently, they *were* capable of muffling the magic coming from themselves – both by their own willpower and augmented with various drugs – to the point where the Beast could barely detect it. But nothing disguised it fully. Traces still leaked out. And the reduction was never enough to make the Beast disappear."

Zeke looked away. I glanced to him, my brow drawing down.

"The electricity in the water," he said. "How we could barely feel it after what those bastards gave you. After what they did."

I trembled. The Sylphaen had said something like that. Something about needing me weak. It was why they'd been fine with hurting me, why they'd given me the neiphiandine.

They'd wanted to keep me from drawing something to them…

And meanwhile, I'd just been so scared, I'd wanted to disappear. To hide from everything down in the tiniest hole I could find.

All of which might have saved my life from the Beast.

"The physicians' tests showed the neiphiandine had suppressants in it," Zeke continued. "They weren't sure why."

My stomach twisted.

"You didn't answer my question," Noah snapped. "That wizard guy. Won't he just try to kill her too?"

"Probably not," Dave answered.

Noah scoffed. "No. No *way* we're going anywhere on a

'probably not'."

"Joseph has a vested interest in this too," Dave said. "He–"

"You sound like you've talked to him," Olivia interrupted.

Dave hesitated. "We email."

She stared. "He refused to speak to any of us after the incident in '98."

"I-I know. He made an exception."

"An *exception?*" Olivia repeated incredulously. "And you never felt the need to report–"

"Everyone treats him like an artifact to be studied! He hates it when people do that!"

Olivia looked like she couldn't decide whether to be furious or laugh.

"Joseph needs this," Dave insisted. "The Beast was targeted at his kind. No matter what he's done since then, if it wakes further – *when* it wakes further – it'll come for him too. And he's our best shot. If anybody can reproduce the originals' solution, it's him."

I swallowed. "But what will that mean for me?"

"You become one or the other. Landwalker or dehaian."

A breath left me.

"But what about *us?*" Ellie asked. "The… the changing back. Being dehaian. If Chloe–"

"That was never going to happen, Ellie," Olivia interrupted, a pained note in her voice. "I know you want that, but over time you would have realized the truth like we have. We're too human. We've *been* too human for centuries and the traces left in us from our ancestors are too minute. None of us would survive a transformation back to the way we once were."

Ellie stared at her. "We could try," she said in a tiny voice.

The pitying look I'd seen at the house returned to the woman's eyes. "It can't be, Ellie. I'm sorry."

Desperately, Ellie turned to Dave. His expression was the same as Olivia's, though tinged with an awkwardness as if he wished the girl wouldn't stare at him like that.

Ellie dropped her gaze to the ground.

"None of this means he won't try to kill her," Noah argued. "He might decide killing her is the best way to get the Beast to disappear."

"That energy release thing," Baylie said, her voice weak. "Won't he know about that, though?"

Noah's brow furrowed.

"Kill me, it releases more of whatever the Beast feeds on," I explained, my own voice not much stronger than Baylie's. I glanced to Zeke. "I think that's what the Sylphaen are after. They must believe they can use it to make themselves like me. But it'll just give the Beast more power." I hesitated. "I don't think they know that part."

Dave shook his head. "Joseph wouldn't risk it."

Silence fell at the words and, from what I could gauge of the others, they had no more idea what to say than I did. We had to do something. We had to stop this somehow.

But this was the guy who created the greliarans. This was the guy who *designed* them to kill us. To trust him with my life, after everything else that'd happened and all the ways 'trusting someone' had gone so wrong…

"It'd stop the Sylphaen," Zeke murmured, his gaze on the cave floor.

I looked over to him.

"And if you… if you became fully landwalker, then Harman would leave you alone," he continued in the same tight tone.

"Maybe," Baylie cautioned.

Zeke gaze's rose to mine. "You could be safe."

My chest quivered at the pain in his eyes.

"But what…" Baylie tried. "What would you *be*? I mean…"

I glanced to her, reading the anxiety in her tone. I could become dehaian – *new* dehaian, like Zeke – and be unable to leave the ocean because of it. I could visit her, but only if she moved to California like Noah. Only if she was within a few miles of the shore.

And speaking of Noah and Zeke…

"You'll have time to think about it on the way," Dave told me. "Joseph's up on the northern California coast. It's quite a drive." He paused, looking to Olivia. "If we're sending them, that is?"

"Letting her go back to the coast is dangerous," Olivia argued.

"But it could solve this," Dave countered. "Keeping her underground won't."

"You're sending them alone?" Ellie asked.

Dave and Olivia glanced to her.

"What if Noah's right and this guy… I don't know, gets upset having Chloe there or–"

"It'll be fine," Dave said. "I'll call him. Let him know they're–"

"But why don't we just go too?" the girl interjected hurriedly, like she was afraid she wouldn't get the words out. "We could, you know, have Chloe help us get there. If she wants to, I mean. Or we could take those medicines."

Olivia regarded her. "Those medicines are dangerous, Ellie. People have died from the side effects, and there's no need for that desperate of action here. And as for Chloe… it's an unnecessary gamble of our safety and hers. We don't know anything about this."

"But the Beast is out there," Ellie implored. "If something goes wrong and you could've helped…"

The woman paused. Her gaze flicked to me, considering. Questioning.

I looked away. This was insane. I didn't know what I'd done to let Zeke come inland with me; it'd just happened. But while Ellie had a point – and maybe it *would* be better for the elders to come since they knew Joseph – doing anything *remotely* non-human worried me right now. And as for the rest of it…

I couldn't be a landwalker. Baylie had been right; all the craziness of the past few weeks aside, I loved the ocean. And to *never* be able to see it again… it was too much to bear.

And that wasn't the only thing…

My gaze skidded across the floor. I couldn't quite bring

myself to look at Zeke or Noah. If I was a dehaian, it didn't really affect anything where they were concerned, which meant the questions about them both were still out there. But it also meant all the other issues would disappear. To some extent, in any case.

And that counted. A lot.

I nodded, trying to show no hint of how sickened I felt. "Okay, yeah," I agreed. "Let's go."

Olivia led the way from the cave, while Dave reluctantly trailed her. Staying close to me and Baylie, and managing to keep a distance from each other at the same time, Noah and Zeke were a bit slower to follow.

I glanced around when we left the shelter of the curve in the mountainside, hoping Chief Reynolds was still on the wild goose chase that Olivia described. I'd be happy if I never saw that man again.

Nothing moved in the forest and Noah gave no sign of hearing anything beyond birds. The trail continued downward, following a steep path from the cave opening. The ground was rough even on the trail, with rocks and depressions where rain had worn away the soil. Keeping my footing was nearly as difficult as it'd been when we were forging through the under-brush, though, really, my shoes didn't help. I was tempted to remove them and let the soles of my feet change enough to handle the terrain, but that'd probably just freak Baylie out.

And there was no telling what could send more energy to the Beast.

I swallowed, working not to think about it. We'd get to this Joseph guy, and then the Beast wouldn't be a problem. Eventually, anyway. I remembered Ellie saying something about how, even after the landwalkers and dehaians had split, it'd taken time for the Beast to lose energy and fall asleep or whatever it was the creature had done. But still… we were making progress.

It'd be fine.

A cacophony of buzzing rose from Ellie's phone, the alerts tripping over one another to be heard, and I nearly jumped out of my skin. Looking startled as well, the girl came to a stop and tugged the cell from her pocket.

Her brow furrowed. "Same number. There's like ten missed calls from when we were in the cave."

The alerts stopped. She looked up at us, appearing confused.

Another buzz came from the phone.

"Oh good grief," Baylie said, leaning over to glance at the screen.

She blinked, and then her gaze rose to me. "It's your mom and dad."

"What?" I asked.

Ellie tilted the phone toward me.

Mom and Dad's number stared back at me.

Baylie made an incredulous noise. "How'd they get Ellie's—"

"Give that here," Olivia interrupted.

Ellie handed the cell to Olivia. The woman regarded the buzzing phone for a moment before thumbing it on.

"Hello?"

She paused.

Noah's brow rose, alarm written across his face, and his gaze snapped to me.

Fear made my stomach quiver. Whatever he heard, that look couldn't mean it was good.

"I believe you have the wrong–" Olivia's brow drew down. "Say that again."

Noah looked like he wanted to grab the phone away from her.

Olivia lowered the cell and covered the speaker with her hand. She turned to me, her expression taut with careful control. "The person on the other end claims he knows you."

I waited, confused.

"He says his name is Wyatt. He…" Olivia's brow furrowed as though she couldn't believe her own words. "He says that he and his family have your parents… as their hostages."

Ice shot through me.

"He insists upon speaking with you."

She extended the cell.

My gaze flicked to Noah. To Zeke. The greliarans had my parents. My crazy, hysterical, backstabbing parents.

Noah's homicidal relatives had my parents.

My hand trembled as I took the phone.

"Hello?" I managed.

"Hey, pretty."

I could hear the grin in Wyatt's voice and picture it on his face. Lascivious slime practically dripped from his tone, and spikes crept from my forearms at the sound.

"What do you want?"

He chuckled. "Here's how it's going to go. We have your mommy and daddy. They're in the back, and they've been there for about a day. I can't say it's going well. So you're coming to us. You're going to give yourself up – you and the other scum-sucker – and we'll let them go. Get it?"

I couldn't breathe and at my silence, the chuckle came again.

"Now, it's no good being all quiet like that. I want to know I have your attention."

A rustling came from the other end of the phone, and then a muffled shriek.

"Talk," I heard Wyatt order in the background. "It's your little fish."

"C-Chloe?" Dad gasped.

A choked noise left me.

"Chloe, don't listen to him. Just get–"

I flinched as his words cut off with a pained sound.

"You there?" Wyatt asked.

I was shaking so much it hurt. "Yes."

"Good. So this part is what I like to call our 'leverage'. We're taking your parents on a bit of a joyride. Today we're in Wyoming. Tomorrow we'll be home on the Washington coast.

And you know what happens to their kind if they get too close to the sea. So you come as fast as you can from wherever it is you're hiding, and maybe I won't throw them into the ocean. You get me? I've heard *all* sorts of stories about what happens to landwalkers when they touch seawater. Skin peeling off, blood pouring out, their heads just–"

"Stop it!" I snapped.

His smile carried through his voice again. "Where are you?"

I hesitated. Noah shook his head hard.

"You hear me, pretty?" Wyatt prompted.

"Arkansas," I answered, giving him the first state name that came to mind.

"Well, then, we'll see you on the coast. Just ask Noah where to go. I'm sure he's there with you."

"Don't hurt them," I whispered.

He laughed. The phone clicked and the line went dead.

A ragged gasp escaped me.

Noah grabbed the phone. "Chloe, you–"

"What happened?" Zeke demanded.

I swallowed hard. "Th-they have my parents. They're taking them to the coast."

Zeke looked away, swearing.

"You can't go after them," Noah insisted.

I shook my head. Breathing was difficult and the ground kept trying to spin beneath me. I knew he was right. Logically, rationally, Noah was right. It'd be suicide.

The idea of what could happen if Wyatt threw Mom and

Dad into seawater flashed through my head.

I felt like I was going to throw up.

"I can't let him hurt them," I managed. "I-I know what Mom and Dad did. What they'd try to do a second time if they could…"

Shivers rattled through me. I hated them. I didn't want to go anywhere near them, and if I never saw them again…

Funny how that idea had never included 'because they were dead'.

"I-I can't," I repeated. "Wyatt and the others are on their way to the ocean. They'll be there by tomorrow. If I don't go–"

"He'll *kill* you," Noah snapped. "And chances are, he'll kill them too."

"Chloe, we have to call the cops," Baylie insisted. "Harman's connections *can't* go all the way–"

"Chief Reynolds said all the other elders agreed with Harman," I countered. "What if they're in this too?"

"We could still try!" Baylie cried.

"I believe the chief was lying," Olivia added. "Or Harman was. I can't imagine *all* the elders would support what he did."

"See?" Noah argued. "Come on, Chloe. Cops, FBI, *something*. You can't just go in there and–"

"They'll throw them in the ocean," I told him. "That's what Wyatt said. They'll throw my parents into the ocean." I turned to Olivia and Dave. "What happens? If they do that to a landwalker, what…"

I could see the answer on their faces. My head shook of its

own accord. "I can't let them. Mom and Dad are probably already sick. If I don't get them away from the coast in time–"

"Could she help them?" Zeke interrupted, directing the question at the elders.

They appeared confused.

"The projection thing we talked about," he continued to Ellie. "How she got me here. Can it really work both ways?"

"You can't *seriously* be arguing that Chloe go there?" Noah snapped, glaring at Zeke.

Zeke ignored him. "Can it?"

Olivia's brow furrowed. "Yes… possibly."

A breath escaped me.

"Hey!" Noah pressed. "You're *not* sending Chloe to them, get it? I won't–"

"I know that," Zeke retorted. "I'm going."

I stared at him.

Noah made an incredulous noise. "Those guys will tear you apart. *Literally.* If anyone's going, then I'll be the one who–"

"Second they see you, they'll kill her parents. You–"

"So what're you planning to do? Those are *greliarans*. 'Created to kill you', remember? You won't stand a–"

"And you will? One against–"

"Enough!"

My shout rang through the forest and at it, they both fell silent. I swallowed, glancing around. Anyone could have heard that. Yelling had been stupid.

I wasn't sure I cared.

"You're not doing this on your own," I told them, my voice and body trembling. "Either of you."

They both hesitated, looking as though they wanted to continue arguing.

"I mean it!" I snapped.

Still shaking, I turned away, my gaze skipping across the forest while my heart raced. I wasn't sure what to do. We had no weapons – nothing but an empty shotgun in the trunk, anyway – and we were up against a bunch of greliarans who knew we were coming and who probably had a strategy for tearing us apart. It didn't matter, though. I refused to allow Zeke or Noah to get themselves killed.

There had to be another solution.

"We'll think of something on the way," I said, looking back at them. "Alright? We'll all work together and we'll come up with a plan."

Without waiting for their response, I turned to Olivia and Dave. "How far is it to the cars?"

Dave twitched his head toward the path, not taking his eyes from me. "About five miles."

"Good," I continued. "Then come on."

Pushing past the others, I strode down the trail. I didn't care what Noah or Zeke said. How horrible those greliarans were. I wouldn't lose them. Either of them, or anyone else for that matter.

Not if there was a thing left on Earth that I could do about it.

9

WYATT

On the back porch, I listened to the waves as they tumbled toward the shore. The air was cool from the wind coming off the ocean, and the sun was still a couple hours shy of rising. Shadows surrounded me, cast from the forest around our house, though moonlight shone down on the sand and the water, making even the gray grit of the beach seem brilliant in the night.

We'd gotten home a little while ago and tossed her parents into the basement before Clay and Owen trudged off to bed. Dad had stayed in the front room – listening to her parents or watching for her, I didn't know.

But I couldn't sleep. Anticipation for what would happen when the fish finally arrived would barely let me close my eyes.

The breeze picked up, strengthening the salt in the air. I drew a deep breath. It felt better, being back on the coast compared to where we'd been. Like I wasn't stretched between here and someplace else anymore. Like some weird tension inside me was gone.

Not that I'd ever admit that to my brothers.

She'd get here soon, though. She'd probably drive like the wind, given how scared she'd seemed on the phone.

My lip twitched. Damn, I'd loved the sound of that.

I couldn't wait to see her face as well.

My smile grew and I struggled to keep it under control. Arkansas *was* a long way from here. I had to be a *little* patient.

Drawing another breath, I scanned the beach.

Three guys were walking along the sand.

My brow furrowed. There wasn't another house near us for miles. That was part of the deal with the landwalkers. We stayed isolated, got to do what we wanted here, and random people didn't wander onto our property.

In swim trunks. And no shirts. With wet hair like they'd just come from the water.

A shiver crept over my skin like it wanted to change. Dehaians. I would've bet money, even if I couldn't believe it. There was something weird about them too. Something off, just like there'd been with her or that black-haired guy.

My shivering grew stronger. After all these years, dehaians had just walked onto–

One of the guys paused, bringing the other two to a stop, and even if I couldn't see his eyes glowing, he still studied the yard like he'd spotted me in the shadows.

He jerked his head at the other two and then cautiously walked closer.

My heart was racing. I had to let them get close. Dehaians were fast. Faster than us, the bastards. And there were three of them. I needed to wait till they didn't stand a chance of escaping.

"Hey," the guy called as he walked up. His tone was guarded, but strangely dismissive too, like he was used to being listened to whether he gave a damn about the conversation or not.

"Yeah?" I managed.

"We're looking for some people. Maybe you've seen them? A guy. Dark hair, blue eyes, about my height. A girl too; teenager with red hair. Their names are Zeke and Chloe, though they might be going by something else now."

Surprise brought everything else to a halt.

"They're runaways," the guy continued. "And criminals. Dangerous ones. There's evidence they came ashore several miles from here after their boat crashed. Have you seen them?"

I stared at him. This couldn't be happening.

How many people had those fish pissed off?

I struggled to push the thought aside. I needed to be smart here. This was more complicated than some dumbass dehaians wandering onto our property. These guys were looking for the same scale-skins as us. They might have others looking too, elsewhere, and maybe I could convince him to bring them to the house as well.

Then we'd have even more of them to kill. More than we ever could have *dreamed*.

A smile twitched across my face before I could stop it.

"Hey? You hear me?" the guy asked.

"Yeah," I responded, trying to think fast. "I, uh–"

The door flew open behind me. I barely stopped my skin from changing in shock.

"You're looking for them?" Dad demanded, striding outside.

The first guy paused, looking more wary than alarmed, though the other two behind him seemed a heartbeat shy of growing spikes in surprise.

"Yeah," the guy said.

"Well, we've seen them," Dad replied. "That son of a bitch killed my son."

The scale-skin's brow rose.

"You want to find them," Dad continued. "So do I. Maybe we can help each other."

I looked to Dad in confusion. Help? Wait, why did he think we needed this scum-sucker's *help*?

The guy made a noncommittal sound.

"Anyone else with you?" I asked into the silence, glancing to the beach and struggling to keep the hope from my tone.

The guy's gaze flicked from me to Dad. "They're around."

"Good," Dad replied. "They can meet us here."

He jerked his chin to the house.

The guy didn't move. "Why'd Zeke kill your son?"

Dad paused. "The girl. He thought Brock was a threat to her."

The scale-skin seemed to consider the words. "And what makes you think they'll come back here?"

I looked to Dad. We couldn't tell him about her parents.

Hostages sort of destroyed the whole 'wounded family' thing Dad had going.

"Because we're close to the girl's parents," Dad said. "So she called us yesterday. Told us she'd convinced him to come back so she could see her mom and dad."

The guy's eyes narrowed.

"We've known them for a while," Dad added darkly. "They want to get her away from him. But that guy is dangerous. They felt safer meeting her here. I want your help making sure he doesn't hurt anyone else."

For a moment, the fish regarded us, and from something in his face, I could tell he didn't believe a word of what Dad had said.

But he wasn't leaving either. He was simply studying us, like he didn't care that we were lying, that we were half again his weight, or that he was standing on our territory. Instead, he was just fitting us into some kind of plan in his head.

"The girl's really coming back here?" he asked.

"What I said, isn't it?" Dad drew a breath, clearly trying to calm down. "I guarantee it."

The guy's brow shrugged. "Alright," he agreed with a brief glance to his companions. "We'd be happy to help."

"Great," Dad retorted. "Then I'm Richard. This is Wyatt. Nice to meet you and all that."

The guy's lip twitched like he found Dad's anger amusing. "Nice to meet you too," he replied dryly. "I'm Niall."

10

ZEKE

I hadn't been on many car rides in my life, but this had to be one of the most uncomfortable and awkward.

And Ellie wasn't even here.

I grimaced. That wasn't fair. The girl was edgy as hell on a good day, but she'd been getting better. She'd barely hesitated when she'd taken my hand in the cave, and she'd trusted me to guide her through the dark.

Least I could do was not make a joke of her, even to myself.

But it *was* uncomfortable in here.

I scrubbed a hand across my tired eyes, trying to stop their burning, and then glanced to the seat beside me. On the other side of the car, Noah was finally asleep. Baylie was the same in the passenger seat ahead of him, while Chloe was driving.

It'd taken hours, and even now, I couldn't be sure Noah was unconscious. Or that he'd stay that way.

Greliaran hearing was infuriating.

Scowling briefly, I unfastened my seat belt and then scooted forward, watching him from the corner of my eye. He didn't stir.

"Chloe," I whispered.

She gasped, flinching.

I winced. "Sorry."

"What's wrong?"

"Nothing," I replied, the word mostly a lie. A ton of things were wrong, running the gamut from the greliaran who wanted the girl I cared about, to the Sylphaen that might be on the coast, to the *other* greliarans we *knew* were there and who had her parents. And that didn't even get into the past few days and the questions I had about that time.

Damn near everything was wrong, if I wanted to be honest about it.

"I just need to talk to you," I continued.

She grimaced, her eyes on the road. The eastern sky was finally shifting toward a lighter shade of indigo, but the night hadn't quite given up its grip on the road. Up ahead, the tail-lights of Olivia's car still glowed red, leading the way as they had for the entire night of driving.

"Not right now, Zeke."

"Then when?"

Chloe gave an awkward shrug, like she was trying to pull away even if there was nowhere to go, and her gaze twitched to Noah before returning quickly to the highway. "I-I can't. I just… I have to focus."

I glanced over. The guy still appeared to be asleep.

Though of course he could be pretending.

"I understand that," I assured her, turning back. "But Chloe, I need to know… did something happen while I was at that lab? Something with you?"

She hesitated.

"It's just," I continued, "when I was there, the pain of my distance from the ocean came back. Not fully, but pretty strong for a while. And I… I can't help but think about what Ellie said. How it wouldn't do that as long as… well, as long as you were alive."

She tightened her hands on the steering wheel. I couldn't tell if she was breathing.

"Chloe?"

"Yeah," she whispered. "Yeah, it was bad."

A shiver ran through me, whether of nausea, horror, or the desire to hit something, I couldn't be sure. My hand slipped from the back of the seat to her shoulder. She tensed.

"Please," she said, her voice choked. "I-I need to drive."

I grimaced, taking my hand away.

An exit sign flashed past and ahead of us, Olivia's car moved to leave the highway. Chloe followed them. At the end of the ramp, the vehicles paused briefly before taking a right toward an enormous gas station situated beside the road. Semi-trucks were arrayed to one side of the concrete sea like a mismatched army, and cars were parked closer to the station or stopped beneath the gas pump shelter fronting it all. Lights glowed over the parking lot like miniature suns while, blinking brightly from the top of a towering pole, a sign flashed various prices for fuel.

When Olivia pulled up beside a gas pump, Chloe came to a stop behind her. With quick motions, she put the car into park and then took the key from the ignition.

She fled the car before I could say a word.

Noah stirred in the other seat.

Ignoring him, I opened the door and went after Chloe.

Striding fast, she headed into the gas station, and I sped up, trying to catch her. When I glanced back, I could see Ellie climbing from Olivia's car and staring after us both, while Dave was focused on filling up the gas tank.

But Noah hadn't tried to follow yet.

Good.

The sliding door hissed open ahead of me, and a blast of air conditioning made the hairs on my arms stand on end. I scanned the brilliantly lit interior, spotting her several aisles from the entrance.

Her gaze twitched my way when I came closer, and she grimaced. "Zeke, I can't–"

"Chloe, stop. Please. I… Are you okay now? Can you at least tell me that?"

She hesitated and then nodded. "Yeah. I'm fine." She paused again. "A-are you?"

My brow furrowed. She made a halting gesture to my forearms.

The confusion cleared and my mouth tightened. I hated the fact she'd seen that.

"Yeah." I took a breath, pushing the frustration away. "Listen, I know you're worried about your parents. We'll help them. But you don't need to–"

"It's not just that."

I paused.

She cast a quick look around. No one was in the station, except for a bored-looking cashier by the register and a pair of truckers sitting in a booth against the far wall, neither of whom glanced away from their pizza.

But Noah was climbing from the car. I fought back a scowl.

Chloe saw him too. "I just don't want to talk right now," she finished, her voice dropping to a whisper.

"Did you kiss him?"

She blinked. "What?"

My heart was pounding, the words having taken me as much by surprise as they did her. And I was being stupid. I shouldn't have said anything, not when she was already so upset. But with the guy right outside and with me never having a chance to talk to Chloe where he wouldn't hear…

I couldn't have stopped myself if I tried.

"Did you?" I pressed. "On the porch the other–"

"You were *watching* us?"

"I was watching the street. I was trying to keep you safe."

A breath left her and she turned away.

"Chloe…"

"No," she snapped. "No, I didn't. And I–" She cut off with an exasperated noise and took off deeper into the store.

I grimaced. Stupid. Stupid, stupid, *stupid*.

And more relieved than I wanted to admit.

Still cursing myself for being an idiot, I followed her.

"Zeke," she warned, her eyes on the racks of snack foods in front of her. "I don't–"

"I'm sorry."

She paused.

"I'm sorry," I repeated.

A heartbeat passed. "Thank you for watching the street," she acknowledged without looking at me.

"Of course."

"You should've gotten sleep."

I hesitated, unsure how to take that. I wasn't going to leave her up by herself, no matter what the others had decided to do.

At my silence, she glanced toward me, though she wouldn't meet my eyes. "It's just… you have to take care of yourself too. I don't–" She seemed to struggle with the words. "I don't want anything to happen to you."

I paused, knowing I couldn't agree to that. Not if it left her at risk. I reached out, taking her hand.

Air left her. For a moment, she closed her eyes, the tension seeming to leak from her.

And then she drew a breath, pulling her fingers from mine. "Please," she said.

Without another word, she snagged a bag of pretzels from the shelf and headed for the register. The cashier rang up her order, regarding us both with a trace of humor the entire time, as though our quiet argument through the aisles had been the most entertainment he'd had all night. Ignoring him completely, Chloe grabbed her change and the pretzels, and strode out of the store.

Noah was waiting by the car. "Everything alright?" he asked neutrally, his gaze flicking between the two of us.

"Fine," Chloe replied. "How much longer till we reach the house?"

He glanced over as Baylie climbed from the passenger seat. "A few hours."

An annoyed breath escaped Chloe, but she just nodded. She looked to Olivia, Ellie, and Dave. "You guys still doing okay?"

The landwalkers hesitated, and for the first time I registered how tense they all appeared. Olivia and Dave had been trading off driving throughout the past day and night, but the strain on their faces looked more pronounced than that effort would have caused.

Chloe seemed to notice it too.

"I-it kind of hurts," Ellie allowed.

"We should probably attempt your… solution now," Olivia added, careful control in her voice. She glanced to Ellie. "Or else return. I think we've come as far as we can."

Protests surfaced past the pain on Ellie's face. Olivia quelled them with a look.

Chloe's brow rose. "Why didn't you all say something?"

She hurried over to them and then hesitated, as though uncertain what to do. Reaching out, she took Ellie's hand.

A heartbeat passed. The pain on the girl's face cleared. She looked up at Chloe. "What did you do?"

Chloe shook her head, seeming unnerved. "Just… wanted it to stop."

She hesitated, not quite looking back toward me, and then she headed for Olivia and Dave on the other side of the car.

The tension in the two elders seemed to evaporate only moments after Chloe touched their hands.

I heard Baylie let out a breath and when I glanced over, I could see her surprise.

She caught sight of me looking at her, and she blinked, attempting to hide the expression.

Releasing Olivia's hand, Chloe hesitated. "So, um…" Her gaze twitched to the elders and away. "You want to drive, Noah?"

Chloe drew the keys from her pocket and extended them to him, not meeting his eyes either.

He took them without a word.

She headed for the rear door of the car. Baylie gave one look to us and then moved for the back seat as well, leaving me to take her place in the front. By the other vehicle, the landwalkers opened the doors and climbed into their car.

And then it was just me and Noah.

I tried not to grimace as I headed for the passenger seat. This had to change. We'd rescue Chloe's parents, we'd take care of Noah's relatives, and then this *had* to change.

Otherwise, I was going to go crazy.

11

CHLOE

Next time I went across the country, I was taking a plane. I'd never been in one and, honestly, I was more than a bit afraid of them crashing.

But it had to be more comfortable than this. Or at least a faster trip – one that maybe wouldn't require magic tricks.

My stomach twisted. I was glad Ellie and the others weren't sick. That was great. It meant I could probably help Mom and Dad when we found them.

The fact that I apparently had magical powers, that I'd been on display with them in front of everyone, and that I didn't even know what I'd *done*… oh, that was less great by far.

On the seat next to me, Baylie's hand twitched. I looked over at her. Keeping an eye to the guys ahead of us, she curled her fingers quickly through the language we'd developed when we were kids.

You okay? she signed.

I hesitated.

Her hand twitched again. *Not a freak.*

I swallowed, closing my eyes. I loved that sign. Loved her for creating it, back when we were little and my parents had me convinced I was being raised by escapees from an insane asylum. We'd used it back and forth for years, when school was awkward or popular kids made us feel dumb or whenever growing up in Reidsburg left us wondering if we were the biggest losers on the planet.

I was so grateful to see it now.

Glancing back to her, I managed a smile. Her brow rose insistently.

I started to nod, only to pause when I caught Noah looking back at me in the rearview mirror.

My stomach twisted for a whole other reason. I dropped my gaze to my lap.

A heartbeat passed. Baylie tapped the seat beside me. I glanced over again.

What? she asked.

I hesitated. I didn't want to lie.

And the truth was too hard to explain.

I gave a tiny shrug.

Her mouth tightened and then her hand flicked into another sign, aimed at the front seat. *Them?*

Or maybe not that hard after all.

I felt like an idiot. I should be concentrating on my parents—even if really, the possibility of what could happen to them left me so nauseated, I could barely stand it. But all hell could break loose when we reached those creeps' house. Everyone here could be seriously hurt.

I needed to focus on coming up with a plan.

And throughout all the hours of driving, my thoughts had just kept slipping back to the two guys now sitting in the front seat.

It was moronic. My parents could die because of psychos who just wanted to get their hands on me. The whole world could be screwed simply because I'd been born half-dehaian and half-landwalker.

And I couldn't stop thinking about boys. About how I couldn't have both of them. About how, for God knew what reason, life felt like torturing me with two amazing guys and ending us all up in this situation where, no matter what I did, one or all of us were going to get hurt. And there was nothing I could do to fix it. I couldn't even seem to figure out what I was feeling for them anymore. When I was around Zeke, I just felt like I wasn't being fair to Noah. Like I was maybe even *cheating* on Noah. But when I was with Noah, it was *exactly* the same for Zeke. I couldn't find a way out of that, and the result just left me going in circles, unable to be with either of them.

If it wouldn't have been even *more* idiotic, I'd have just burst into tears.

I shrugged again.

Baylie sighed. She probably knew I was lying. All things considered, she was pretty good about that.

But thankfully, she also didn't press for more.

Hours crept by. Portland arrived, with morning commuter traffic everywhere and buildings shining in the sunlight. The highway led us over a river and north past the suburbs, until finally the city fell behind us. Long after the state line had come and gone as well, Noah took an exit from the highway and soon after that, the main roads were a thing of the past. The rumble of gravel beneath the tires became our constant companion while we wound through the maze of back roads, where pines like Christmas trees on steroids formed blinding walls on either side of the car.

I knew we were approaching the coast, though. With every passing mile, my awareness of the ocean was growing stronger. I couldn't see it yet, couldn't even guess how many miles we had left to go. I hadn't seen a house in what felt like forever and the closest we'd come to signs of civilization had been other dirt tracks that twisted into oblivion through the trees.

But we were close, so close it made shivers run over my skin.

Baylie shifted position on the seat beside me and the motion snapped me back to the present. She drew her cell phone from her pocket and then glanced to it. Her brow furrowed at what she saw.

My stomach twisted nervously as I read her expression. We were in the middle of nowhere. If we *did* end up calling the police, it'd be a miracle if they could find us in this mess. Or if we had enough cell signal to reach them.

"So," Baylie prompted, raising her voice over the gravel's

roar. "How much longer?"

"Maybe twenty minutes," Noah answered.

"And when we get there," she continued. "What's the plan?"

Noah's gaze flicked up to the rearview mirror. Zeke turned his head toward us, though he didn't quite look back to me or Baylie.

And that was it.

I drew a slow breath, working to stay calm. They weren't going in there by themselves. That wasn't going to happen.

But this wasn't exactly encouraging either. I hadn't come up with anything, but I'd been hoping someone else had.

"When do you think we should call the cops?" Baylie pressed.

Noah shifted uncomfortably in the driver's seat. "My uncle probably has an arrangement with them. If the landwalkers take care of things for greliarans…" He shook his head. "Let's just say that goes a *long* way toward explaining how my cousins haven't managed to end up in jail by now."

"We need to do something," Baylie argued. "We can't just go in there guns blazing or whatever."

No one said anything.

An annoyed sound escaped her. "Pull over," she ordered.

Noah hesitated, and then did as instructed.

"Okay, listen," Baylie said. "What's the plan? Where will they have the Kowalskis?"

I glanced through the rear window. Olivia was pulling her car over as well.

"Noah?" Baylie pushed.

"I'm not sure," he grudged. "There's a shed to the south of the house, so they could be there. Or the basement. They… they also have traps around the property."

"Traps?" I repeated incredulously.

He paused. "They say they're for animals."

It wasn't hard to read the implication. I swallowed and glanced back again when the doors on Olivia's car shut. The elders started toward us and Ellie trailed after them, giving nervous looks to the forest while she came.

"The pits are pretty deep, though," Noah continued. "They've got grates set up to close over the tops to hold onto whatever gets inside. It'd make a good cage, so it's possible they put your parents in one of those."

"We can't just search through the whole forest," Zeke said.

"Oh, no kidding," Noah retorted.

"Okay," I cut in before they could say anything else.

Olivia stopped beside the window. Noah grimaced and then pushed open the door.

"What's going on?" the woman asked while we all climbed from the car.

"Coming up with a plan," Baylie explained.

Olivia glanced between us, her brow rising expectantly.

Zeke and Noah didn't say anything.

"We should call the cops," Baylie insisted. "They can look for Chloe's parents."

"*If* they believe us," Noah countered.

"They will," Olivia said.

Ellie looked away.

My brow furrowed. I recognized that expression on the girl's face and it made my stomach start to churn again. "Why are you so sure?"

"I've spoken with the other elders," Olivia replied.

Baylie seemed to choke at the words.

"You've *what*?" Zeke demanded.

"I called them from the road. I couldn't imagine they actually sided with Harman, and I was right. A few have. But the rest believe as we do." She nodded to Dave, including him in the comment. "They've given us the information we need to get the police to help us, once we have a place to send them."

I stared at her.

"And the others?" Zeke said. "The ones who *did* 'side with Harman'? What if they hear about this?"

"Robin and Phil are with them. They'll make certain the elders are circumspect in their communications."

I felt like laughing, except nothing was funny. Harman would still find out. Of *course* he'd find out. The crazy little man had been only a few hours behind us in crossing half the *country*, and that time, no one had bothered to send up a signal on where we were.

"Also," Olivia continued. "The elders are on their way. Once this situation is dealt with, they want us to meet them so that they can talk with you."

My eyes went wide. "Wait, *what*?"

"Get Chloe to use what she can do on them, you mean,"

Noah snapped.

Olivia paused.

"I thought what she is attracts that Beast creature," Zeke said. "And now you want her to… what? Throw out flares for the damn thing by using her magic on your friends too?" He made an angry sound. "She's not just some *thing* you can exploit for your benefit."

Noah scoffed, looking like for once he and Zeke were in total agreement.

"We simply wish to talk," Olivia emphasized.

"And the police *will* come if we ask," Dave added like he was trying to appease us. "The other elders have connections out here. They've told us the people to contact for help in dealing with these animals."

His gaze twitched to Baylie, as though he regretted the last word slipping out.

"We'll need to keep Chloe away from the police, however," Olivia said.

My brow drew down. "Why?"

"You were technically viewed as the victim of a kidnapping not too long ago, remember? If the police see you and think of that, they might be more than a bit curious why you're here."

"Your connections can't just explain that away too?" Noah snapped sarcastically.

Her mouth tightened. "They are not *my* connections, so I don't know what other factors might impact their decisions. They will come to help us with these people if we ask. Beyond that, I can't say."

The urge to laugh returned, and I could see the same on Zeke's face. Shaking his head incredulously, he turned away.

"But they *will* arrest them?" Baylie pressed.

Olivia nodded. "I've been assured that the protections afforded to these greliarans will be removed. By the elders who agree with us, at least."

I grimaced. That didn't sound as comforting as she probably intended.

"And what am I supposed to do?" I asked. "Hide in the forest when the cops show up?"

"You stay away from all this. Dave will drive you back toward–"

"What about my parents?"

"We will bring them to you."

I stared at her. "They could die. They could be dead now! No, I'm going."

"You are too important," Olivia objected. "If something happened–"

"I'm not letting them die!"

Zeke winced. "Chloe, they–"

"I'm *not*, Zeke! These are my parents. What if it was your dad and you–"

The words caught up to me and I cut off. I couldn't believe I'd brought that up.

Zeke's face tightened. He looked away.

Noah glanced between us. "It'll be safer if you're not there," he said to me. "If they got their hands on you–"

"I'm *going*," I insisted, tearing my gaze from Zeke to glare at Noah and the elders alike.

Olivia shook her head in exasperation.

"So then what's the plan?" Baylie asked. "We're calling the cops… when?"

It took Olivia a moment to reply. "Sooner would be best. It'll take them time to arrive, regardless. Once they're here, we can go onward to the greliarans–"

"Hold on," I cut in, "you're saying wait? How long will it be till the police get here?"

Olivia hesitated. I looked to Noah, my brow twitching up in tacit repetition of the question.

"A while," he allowed. "I'm not sure."

"Mom and Dad could be dead by then. If I can just get close enough to help them, buy us time till the cops *do* show up–"

"Chloe, you're being irrational," Olivia snapped, annoyance breaking through her voice for the first time. "The police are our *best* chance of dealing with them. We could be hurt or killed if we try to confront these creatures ourselves."

My chest shook with the urge to scream or cry. I knew she was right, about the last part at least. Zeke, Noah, Baylie… any of them could be hurt in this. And that wasn't acceptable. It would never be okay.

But I remembered Mom and Dad after they'd come to get me from Santa Lucina that first time. I remembered how they'd looked when they arrived at the cabin after I'd run away.

Dad had just gotten out of the hospital. Mom seemed barely able to stand.

And now...

"People's lives are at stake," Zeke said quietly.

I blinked, turning to him. He didn't look at me.

"Call the cops," he continued. "We'll go on ahead till they get here."

Noah grimaced, still seeming like he wanted to argue.

Olivia didn't appear much different. "Chloe is too important to risk–"

"She wants to go. She's going. End of discussion."

Zeke's face was like stone and in his voice, I could hear traces of the royal authority he rarely let show through.

Olivia seemed to hear something of it herself. Eyeing him, she straightened as though drawing upon her status as a land-walker elder.

Zeke's expression didn't change.

Her mouth thinned. "Fine," she allowed bitingly. "But we can't *all* go. Someone will need to stay near the main roads to guide the police when they respond to our call. Trusting that they'll find the greliarans in this maze..." She shook her head again and then glanced over. "Dave?"

"Oh, yeah, sure," he agreed to the implicit request.

I fought to keep from rolling my eyes. The man looked like he wanted to take off right now.

"Ellie will stay with him," Olivia continued.

"I–"

The woman pinned her with a sharp glance. Ellie grimaced, turning away.

"And I'll come with you," Olivia continued, "to see if the greliarans can't be reasoned with on the grounds of potentially losing their protection by the elders. As a greliaran, Baylie is an obvious addition to our group, and Noah should follow Dave and Ellie. It'll be safer for a human to be–"

"No," Noah interrupted. "You are *not* sending her–"

"Your stepsister will be able to defend herself against these creatures, Noah, and you won't. I apologize for being so blunt but–"

"No, she can't!" Noah snapped. "I am *telling* you, Baylie is not a damn greliaran!"

The woman gave him a tired look.

Fissures raced through Noah's skin like an accelerated earthquake, and firelight flared to life inside them. His eyes transformed into red-hot coals and when he spoke, his voice was a growl that sent shivers running through me. "*Get it?*"

Olivia swallowed tightly. Ellie stared at him, wide-eyed.

Noah drew a breath. The cracks mended together, taking the glowing light with them, and his eyes became emerald green and human again.

"I would know if she was," he told the woman flatly. "Baylie was reacting to *me* when that cop and his buddies showed up. And she was mad at you for calling us monsters because we're not all that way."

He glanced to the forest ahead of us. "But those guys are. I know. I'm related to them. So while yes, I think you all should head back to the main road and stay out of this, and no, I don't think you stand a chance in hell of *reasoning* with them about *anything*," he looked between Olivia and Dave, "I'd also appreciate it if you stopped treating my stepsister like she's an *animal*."

A heartbeat passed.

"Noah," Baylie started. "I don't want to just stay back there while you all are–"

"Please," he insisted. "They've already tried to hurt you twice."

She bit her lip, her gaze darting between us all. And then she nodded.

"Fine," Zeke agreed. "Then you guys head back and call the police while you're on the way." He glanced to the car. "I'll take the shotgun. It's empty, but maybe they won't realize that. And you stay between us."

He directed the last to me and I nodded. Noah did the same when Zeke looked to him.

"We'll go to the house," Zeke continued. "There's no point in sneaking through the forest when we don't know where her parents are and the greliarans can hear us coming anyway. We'll see if we can convince your relatives to bring them out, and get Chloe close enough to help her mom and dad. Then it's just a matter of buying time till the police arrive."

"Which might be the hardest part," Noah pointed out.

"Will they kill you?" Zeke asked him.

I looked over in alarm.

Noah paused. "Probably not."

I swallowed, wishing he could have made his response sound more certain than it did.

"Then you cover our retreat if we have to run," Zeke told him.

A moment passed before Noah nodded again.

"Good," Zeke finished. "Let's go."

12

WYATT

Dehaians were inside the house.

Dehaians were everywhere.

And if I didn't get to kill at least *one* of them soon, I was going to go insane.

Fighting back a growl, I paced away from the front room. A trio of scum-suckers had gathered there to watch the road, and their proximity was making me twitch. They didn't seem to know what we were – an ignorance that would've been a pleasure to dispel if not for Dad forbidding us from coming near them. He wanted their help containing that Zeke guy if he tried to escape, and I'd nearly ended up with a broken rib for insisting we could take care of the scale-skin bastard ourselves.

It was insulting. We were working with fish. *Fish*. And sure, Dad promised we'd throw them all in the basement and kill them nice and slow once the guy was dead, but in the meantime…

The growl threatened to come back. In the meantime, I'd spent hours being forced to pretend I was human, while carrying on like we were some grieving family all heartbroken over little Brock. Dad was the only one who didn't seem to be having trouble with the charade, though Clay and Owen appeared pretty content to play along. Countermanding Dad never even *occurred* to them, and when he'd sent them both into the woods a little while ago, ordering them to keep watch, they hadn't even tried to protest.

Dad trusted them too much. Half a dozen scale-skins had gone with each of them, and I wouldn't gamble on the idiots resisting the urge to kill those things for more than five minutes at most.

His whole plan was ridiculous.

As usual.

I shook my head while I made my way down the hall. Past the basement door, I could hear the man and his wife still sniveling quietly. They hadn't looked good last time I checked. Pale and shaking, they'd barely been able to pull away when I nudged them with my foot. The room stank from where one of them had thrown up at some point, and the sweat covering them just added to the stench.

The girl better get here soon. Those two wouldn't last much longer, and while hostages were one thing, bluffing that our leverage still lived was something else entirely.

I reached the end of the hallway and paused. The back room stretched the width of the house, and most of its far wall consisted only of windows. There was almost no furniture, barring the dining table to my right and a few ragged easy chairs near the old television on my left. We rarely spent much time in here, since I preferred eating in my room and none of us cooked for each other anyway. Random discarded objects scattered the tabletop as a result – from old mail to empty dishes – most of them abandoned on trips through the room and then forgotten.

But that Niall guy was in there. Standing by the dinner table, he was watching the ocean past the windows while his hand idly rolled one of Clay's baseballs back and forth across the wooden tabletop. Only half his face was visible to me, and he didn't turn when I stopped by the door. Dehaians didn't have our hearing and I was quiet by default; he probably didn't even know I was here.

I tensed with the urge to rush him. The guy bothered me, even more than the other fish. There was just something off about him. He was cold as hell when the other scale-skins were nearby, and he ordered them around like he was some goddamn king. But when he was alone…

The guy's brow twitched down, a look on his face like he was bothered by something. I eased back into the hall.

When he was alone, he fidgeted with whatever was at hand and stared at nothing like he was chasing something in circles inside his head.

It was creepy.

I would have loved to make it stop.

Dad's footsteps thudded on the stairs. Niall turned, that icy arrogance back on his face, and I quickly tried to make it seem like I'd just been walking down the hallway.

"Car's coming," Dad said when he reached the hall.

I looked past him to the door. I didn't hear–

Tires rumbled faintly in the distance.

I started to smile. The expression died at Dad's glare.

Niall strode past me.

My hands flinched and I barely kept myself from grabbing him. He was so close. So goddamn *close*…

The scum-sucker moved off down the hall.

"Keep it together," Dad growled, coming up beside me. "I see you try that again…"

The threat in his voice was more than clear. He'd beaten us to pulps when we were kids and we didn't do things his way. Now that we were older, it hadn't much stopped, though these days, heavy objects usually got involved.

He was bigger, he was stronger, and he damn well knew it. He didn't even look at me again as he turned and walked after Niall.

I shuddered. I hated him. His stupid plans and the way he'd left us stuck here, pretending to be humans with scale-skins all around. There weren't words to describe it. This wasn't how greliarans were meant to behave.

But then, the girl would be dead soon. I'd squeeze the life out of her pretty little fish body and I'd finally get to feel that magic rushing into me. Putting up with that muscle-bound jackass for all these years would almost be worth it once that happened.

Working to keep my hands from shaking, I followed him to the door.

13

CHLOE

The dense forest made me feel like I was trapped in a tunnel of green with monsters at the end.

Which was mostly true.

In the back seat of Olivia's car, I cast a nervous glance ahead of me to Noah for the twentieth time. He'd hidden his presence from his family, though we all knew they'd hear us coming anyway. But maybe, if they didn't hide as well, we'd have some warning of where they were in this mess of evergreen trees.

But so far, there was nothing.

The car came around a turn of the track, and a bit farther on, the road opened up into a clearing. A two-story, cabin-like house of red logs stood to the right of the path, with a raised porch running the length of the building. The green, aluminum-slatted roof blended with the trees, while a matching shed waited to the left of the road.

And beyond it all lay the ocean. The waves crashed into the rocky shore in a turbulent rush, while the sky stretched from

156

here to the horizon in a great swath of bluish-gray haze that ultimately blurred into the sea.

In spite of everything, I shivered with longing, and from the corner of my eye, I saw Zeke shift a bit. I glanced to him. One hand steadying the shotgun that was propped upright beside his legs, he blinked and tugged his gaze from the sea.

It'd been so long. I'd felt the ocean this entire time, and knew we were getting close, but seeing it again…

I drew a breath, forcing myself to concentrate while Olivia pulled the car to a stop. Being near the water was dangerous. The moment I used any magic to help my parents, the Beast could figure out I was here.

If it didn't know already.

I swallowed hard, attempting to ignore that thought while I scanned the property.

Nothing moved.

We climbed from the car. Birds called in the trees. Wind blew from the ocean, carrying the smell of salt and making my skin want to change.

My focus snapped back when the front door opened, its sound loud in the stillness of the clearing.

Niall walked onto the porch.

I felt like someone had punched me in the stomach. His face was cold when he looked at us and his brilliant blue eyes were the same. Behind him, Wyatt and a man who could only be the guy's father emerged from the house. I could see Wyatt shaking from the urge to race at us, though every few heartbeats, his attention twitched toward Niall like he could barely keep from attacking him too.

Niall's gaze flicked to him, as if noting the shaking as well, though his expression didn't change.

"Hello Zeke," he said, looking back to us again.

Zeke's jaw muscles jumped. "Niall."

"We're just here for Chloe's parents," Noah called, scanning the clearing.

I followed his gaze nervously, realizing that the other two greliarans were nowhere to be seen.

Wyatt chuckled. "Yeah, well, sure." He grinned at me. "Come on, pretty. You and your friend join us over here, and we'll let little Noah have your parents."

Heart pounding, I looked past him to his father. "Let me see them. I want to know they're okay."

The man paused, considering.

"What?" Wyatt mocked. "You don't trust us?"

I swallowed, watching his dad. "Please," I added carefully.

The man's lip twitched. "Wyatt," he snapped, not taking his eyes from me. "Go get them."

His son gave him an incredulous glance.

"Now," the man ordered.

Wyatt's mouth spasmed toward a snarl, but he went.

Seconds crept past. I took a shaky breath, my gaze sliding toward the ocean. It seemed unchanged.

A door slammed in the house. My heart climbed my throat at the sound of shuffling.

Mom and Dad came out the door with Wyatt behind them. They were hardly walking. They could barely even stand. Their faces were white as ash and their bodies trembled as though the proximity to the ocean was shaking them apart. Clutching each other for stability, they stumbled across the porch till their hands landed on the stairway banister.

I started toward them. Noah caught my arm, holding me back.

Atop the steps, Mom spotted me. Her eyes went wide and her grip clenched on Dad. "Chloe?"

They tried to hurry down the stairs, nearly tumbling to their knees by the time they made it to the yard. Watching them as though he was enjoying the show, Wyatt sauntered after them. They staggered on for a few more steps and then, with a smirk, he shoved them both forward.

A choked noise escaped me when they fell to the dirt.

"Wyatt!" his father barked.

Still smirking, Wyatt held up his hands and retreated, leaving them in the center of the clearing.

Noah and Zeke stayed with me as I rushed forward. Taking up positions on either side of me, they eyed Wyatt and the others while I dropped to my knees.

"Chloe," Dad gasped. "Go. Get out of–" His words degenerated into a hacking cough.

I grasped their hands. Their skin was cool. Too cool, and their fingers trembled in mine.

My gaze flashed to the water. I prayed that Beast thing

wouldn't feel this.

I closed my eyes, willing them to be okay, for the ocean to stop hurting, for nothing of the sea to cause them pain ever again.

A shiver tingled across my skin, as if it was about to change. I drew a sharp breath, opening my eyes.

Color was returning to their faces. Their trembling faded away. They seemed to be breathing easier than before.

Dad blinked and then looked up at me. "Chloe, what did you do?"

I glanced to the ocean. The waves rolled in under the blue-metal sky, seeming no different than before. The wind carried the salty air past us, feeling no stronger than it had.

Relief rushed through me. I turned back when Mom pushed up from the ground.

"It doesn't hurt," she whispered with amazement. "Nothing… nothing hurts."

"What happened?" Wyatt snapped.

My gaze rose to find him gaping at me with offended rage like I'd stolen his toy. On the porch, Niall stared as if he couldn't decide whether I was an abomination or a prize.

Wyatt's dad cleared his throat. "Take her," he ordered his son, his voice a bit less steady than before. "The boy too."

"That won't be happening," Olivia called, stepping past us quickly. Alarmed, Noah grabbed at her arm to stop her, but she avoided him with barely a glance. Straightening to every inch of her height, she came to a halt between us and the porch stairs, and regarded Wyatt's father with a stern expression.

Wyatt snorted at her. "Oh, really? You gonna stop us?"

Olivia didn't even look at him. "I am here on behalf of your benefactors, Richard," she declared. "Of which I am one. Your protections are in danger of being removed. If you do not allow me to take the entire Kowalski family, Noah, and Zeke out of here unharmed, I will make certain you and your sons find yourselves on a fast track to prison."

Curiosity flickered through Niall's eyes at the words.

"What if we just kill you instead?" Wyatt snapped.

Olivia ignored him.

Richard did as well. "Nice speech," he replied, "considering you have no proof."

"My proof lies in the police who are coming, and the sheriff who will, if we ask, suddenly find himself being paid to arrest you rather than look the other way."

Richard's mouth twitched toward a snarl, though he held it mostly under control. "You're bluffing. I know one *benefactor* who offered us just about anything to get those two back – including her parents. And plenty of others who are invested in his 'research'."

"There are a few," Olivia allowed. "However, the individual who established the arrangement with your local sheriff is not one of them. So tell me… how do you feel about losing your home? Your freedom? How would you like to see your sons in prison over the little 'problems' we've cleaned up for you over the years?"

The man didn't respond. At my side, I saw Noah glance to the forest, his brow flickering down.

"This is bullshit," Wyatt spat into the silence. "We don't need your *protection*, you pathetic, scum-sucker-loving–"

"Shut up, Wyatt," Richard snapped. His gaze twitched to the forest too.

I swallowed. I couldn't hear anything.

That didn't mean much.

"You bring the cops out here," Richard continued, pulling his focus back to us. "You call the sheriff. I'll show them the thing that murdered my son."

Niall glanced from Richard to Zeke, the curiosity in his gaze taking on a tinge of caution.

Olivia shook her head. "We–"

"No!" Richard barked. "My son is dead, so you take your arrangement and you shove it, you hear me?" He gestured sharply to Wyatt. "Get them over here."

Wyatt started forward.

Zeke swung the shotgun up while Noah moved in front of me.

"I'm warning you!" Olivia cried. "I *forbid* you from–"

Wyatt grabbed her and flung her at Zeke.

A shout came from the forest, followed by a roar. A man screamed, the sound cutting short fast, and then another roar rose from behind the trees on the opposite side of the clearing.

Zeke turned to grab me while Olivia stumbled aside. Noah stayed between us and Wyatt, trying to watch both sides of the yard and his cousin all at once.

Two men ran from the forest.

A greliaran chased them. More fissures than I'd ever seen on Noah covered the guy, till he looked like a monster of molten lava that skin could barely hold in human form.

"Trap!" one of the men shouted at Niall. "They're–"

The greliaran caught him, hefted him bodily into the air, and then hurled him back toward a tree, where he hit with a sickening crunch. The other man turned, spikes rushing from his arms.

He followed his companion into the tree trunk.

Niall took one look at Richard and then leapt from the porch to the dirt. Richard started after him, his skin changing.

Another greliaran ran from the woods on the other side of the clearing, in pursuit of more men. When the dehaians reached the yard, they spun to face the creature, spikes extended.

In a single motion, the greliaran grabbed two of them by the throat. Their spikes deflected uselessly from his arms as he lifted them, and his mouth curved into a smile while their bodies thrashed and flailed.

Their necks snapped in his hands.

The greliaran shuddered, utter ecstasy slackening his inhuman face. He tossed the bodies aside.

I stared, frozen.

Zeke hauled on my arm, dragging me from the ground.

"Run!" Noah ordered us, his gaze darting from Wyatt to the other greliarans.

Olivia wasted no time; she grabbed my mother by one elbow and my father by the other. "Get up!" she commanded, watching the greliarans.

Mom and Dad scrambled to their feet.

Wyatt roared and charged at Noah, slamming into him and driving him back toward us. Olivia and my parents tumbled aside, barely managing to get out of the way, while Zeke pulled me to him and away from their path.

Motion caught the corner of my eye. I turned.

Niall lunged at me.

Zeke twisted, trying to push me aside and block him.

Niall drove his fist into his brother's stomach, and a choked noise escaped Zeke when the blow landed hard. Without hesitation, Niall pulled back his other fist and swung at Zeke's face.

Richard snagged Niall's arm. Snarling like a wild animal, he took Niall's shoulder with his other hand and then hurled him backwards.

"Get over here, you bastard," Richard growled at Zeke.

Keeping me behind him, Zeke retreated as the man stalked toward us.

"Owen! Clay!" Richard barked at the two other greliarans. "Get the girl!"

I glanced to the yard. There wasn't anywhere to go. Olivia had the keys and we'd never make it to the car anyway. Not all of us. Meanwhile, the surviving dehaians were holding their distance and watching us, as though torn about whether to fight or run. Niall was on the ground, struggling to get back up, and my parents were with Olivia on the other side of Noah and Wyatt's struggle.

And it seemed like Wyatt was winning.

Clay and Owen charged.

Brown balls sped through the air, hitting them each in rapid succession. The impacts drove them to the ground, where vines exploded over them. Ropes like living tentacles crawled across their bodies and dug into the dirt. The greliarans struggled, roaring furiously, but for every rope they snapped, more grew to take its place.

Another pod flew toward us, narrowly missing Noah and striking Wyatt on the shoulder. Wyatt snarled, ripping at the ropes and stumbling away as if to distance himself from the vines racing over his chest. A second pod burst against his legs. Ropes swarmed over him and plunged into the dirt, dragging him to his knees.

I looked to the dehaians and then to the coast, trying to figure out where the shots had come from.

Jirral ran from the ocean, a vest across his chest, knives on the belt at his waist, and his gray hair dripping from the water. In his hands, he held a weapon like a stone shotgun and as I watched, he took aim to fire again.

Niall glanced from us to his grandfather, and then he shoved to his feet and raced for the forest.

Pods slammed into the trees near him when he darted past. Around the clearing, the other dehaians retreated quickly, melting into the woods.

Richard stared at Jirral for a heartbeat, rage painted across his crack-ridden face.

And then he lunged for Zeke.

A barrage of nets drove him to the ground.

Jirral swung the gun toward Noah.

"No!" I yelled.

Jirral pulled the weapon up short, not firing.

In the surf behind him, Ina appeared. A slim, leather-like bag was slung over her shoulder and at her hips, a sheathed knife hung from a thin belt. Scales vanished from her legs while she ran through the waves toward us, though dark silver swirls still twisted down her skin from her gunmetal swimsuit, as though she wasn't paying attention to whether they disappeared. Racing past her grandfather, she ignored the greliarans still snarling on the ground while she sped barefoot across the rocky yard.

She threw her arms around Zeke, holding him tight for a moment before pushing away to examine at him. "Are you alright?" she demanded. "Did they hurt you?"

He looked from her to Jirral. "I'm fine. What are you two doing here?"

"Searching for you," his grandfather answered. "We've been tracking those boys with Niall, in case they came across you first. We lost them for a bit, but we spotted one taking off through the water like sharks from hell were on his tail a few minutes ago." His brow shrugged. "Figured you might be involved."

"What, um… what are these…" Ina began, glancing to Noah warily.

"Later," Jirral interrupted. "We need to move. Niall's guys might come back."

Several yards away, Wyatt shoved to his feet, the final ropes snapping from him. Jirral pulled something from a pocket of his vest, slammed it into the back of the gun, and then fired again at the guy.

Nets exploded over Wyatt, driving him back to the ground.

"And these things won't stay down forever," Jirral added.

Zeke swallowed, his arm still around Ina.

"And who would you be?" Olivia asked, pushing to her feet and then brushing the dirt from her jeans. Behind her, Dad helped Mom stand while he watched the greliarans and the dehaians warily.

"Jirral. This is my granddaughter, Ina." Jirral glanced from Olivia to Zeke, as though questioning how much more he needed to explain.

"My sister," Zeke supplied.

"Well, Jirral, I agree," Olivia said. "We need to go. The police will be here soon. We need to get Chloe out of here before they arrive."

"Why does Chloe need to hide from the police?" Mom asked, alarmed.

Olivia's mouth thinned. She didn't respond, but instead turned to Noah. "If you'd please take the Kowalskis to my car?"

Noah hesitated. I looked to the vehicle, and then to Jirral and Ina, reality catching up to me. They couldn't come with us. There wasn't enough room for them in the car. There would've been barely enough room with my parents and the people we'd already brought.

And I couldn't go in the water. I was already too close.

But Zeke could.

We had to split up. If Ina and Jirral were going to follow us to Joseph's – since I doubted they'd agree to simply head home now that they'd found Zeke again – we had no choice.

My stomach roiled. I didn't want to do this. But there wasn't another option, short of having Zeke leave his family behind.

Again.

"Is it safe out there?" I asked Jirral, working to hold my voice steady.

Zeke turned to me in alarm. I didn't look away from his grandfather.

"It's a bit crowded," Jirral allowed. "Ren's got soldiers everywhere. Mercenaries have been prowling around too, though obviously they're staying out of the soldiers' sight." He paused. "Pretty sure they're all looking for you both."

My stomach grew worse. I turned to Zeke.

"Chloe," he protested, reading the look in my eyes. "I'm not–"

"Guide them to Joseph's, okay? Just… follow the directions Dave gave us."

He didn't respond. My brow rose pleadingly.

A breath left Zeke.

"We need to go," Olivia pressed. "*Now.* Even being this close to the water is dangerous."

Zeke's gaze flicked over, regarding her, and then it went to my parents. To Noah.

And then me.

"We'll meet you," he said to me, nothing but certainty in his tone. "We'll probably even get there before you."

I nodded, attempting to look confident and not think about the mercenaries. The Sylphaen. The Beast.

He reached out, taking my hand. "See you soon."

"You too," I replied.

"Go on," he continued to the others. "We'll make sure they don't follow."

He twitched his head at the greliarans.

My parents wasted no time in hurrying toward the car. Olivia hovered by me, looking ready to pull me after them.

"Soon," I repeated to Zeke.

He nodded. A tingle of aveluria magic brushed my palm like a kiss, making my breath catch.

And then his fingers dropped from mine. Swallowing hard, I hesitated. We had to go. I knew it.

I just couldn't shake the sudden fear crawling up my spine.

Unsteadily, I tried for a smile and then turned, walking toward the car while Richard and his sons struggled to break free around me. Noah stayed by my side, watching his family and Zeke's alike.

Owen broke the ropes. Jirral fired another barrage of pods at him, binding him back to the ground.

I climbed into the passenger seat, not looking away from Zeke while worry bounced around in my chest like a trapped bird. I'd see him again. He'd be fine. The Sylphaen and his brother and the whole damn world aside, he'd be fine.

Olivia started the engine while Noah got in next to my parents in the back. The car reversed down the lane, and then turned to face the path inland.

In the tiny side mirror, I watched while Zeke and his family took off for the ocean.

14

ZEKE

The change rushed through me when I hit the water, disintegrating my clothes and making my legs vanish into a tail. I couldn't suppress a breath of relief at the feeling. I hadn't realized how much the pressure to change had been building inside me till we'd driven up a short while ago. The urge to get in the water had been nearly overwhelming. And now… now it would have felt amazing.

Except for one thing.

I surfaced and looked back to the shore. Olivia's car was gone, and Chloe with it. The greliarans were breaking free of their restraints, but even if they'd been as fast of runners as us, they still couldn't have caught the sedan.

"Zeke?" Ina called from farther out in the water.

I forced myself to dive beneath the waves. Chloe would be alright. The greliarans were here, the landwalkers were inland, and there wasn't anything between her and Joseph's home. And it wouldn't take us long to get there. I'd see her again soon.

I shivered, trying to make myself believe the words.

"You okay?" Ina asked when I pulled up beside her.

I nodded. "Yeah."

She didn't look convinced, but said nothing more about it.

Jirral circled back toward us. "Clear for now. Where to?"

"South. There's a, um, a guy Chloe needs to see."

"A guy?" Jirral repeated.

"It's a long story. But that half-landwalker, half-dehaian thing… he's going to try to take that away. Make her one or the other." I paused. "We need to meet her. Be with her when that happens."

I watched them, waiting. It wasn't really true that we *had* to be there. As far as I was aware, our presence – *my* presence – wouldn't be crucial to whatever that wizard guy planned to do.

But it also didn't matter. I wasn't going to leave Chloe by herself in this.

And if she ended up landwalker instead of dehaian, a beach surrounded by tentacle-roped greliarans was *not* going to be the last time I ever saw her.

I shuddered. The thought made me feel sick.

"Alright," Jirral agreed cautiously. "Well, stay close and tell me where to go, then."

He started off. Ina and I followed.

"She's half *what?*" Ina asked me quietly.

I glanced over at her, wincing a bit. Landwalkers had been part of the myths and children's stories Dad forbade anyone to teach us, on account of how they weren't 'necessary' for future leaders of Yvaria. And while yes, Jirral had talked about land-walkers that day we met him in his house, he'd said they were a crazy fairy tale in which the Sylphaen believed.

Chloe hadn't mentioned anything about actually being half of one at the time.

"Again," I replied. "Long story."

She paused. "Okay."

We continued on. Waves rolled overhead, growing more distant as we followed the seafloor down. Light faded, though my eyes and my awareness of the water compensated easily. The ocean was mostly empty around us, with only a pod of whales nearby to keep us company, and though the temperature was plummeting as steadily as the ground, magic kept me from feeling it and the water pressure alike.

Smaller forms flitted past the edge of my senses. Jirral slowed.

"Vetorians or soldiers?" Ina whispered.

Jirral didn't respond.

I glanced around, searching for any other signs of mercenaries or Ren's people.

"There are caves a few miles west," Jirral said quietly. "Head there. I'll go check this out."

Ina nodded and took off.

I hesitated. Truth was, as much as I appreciated him shooting the greliarans, I didn't know what was better: having him determine if those dehaians were a threat, or having him watch Ina while I checked.

Either meant trusting him.

And that wasn't the only thing.

"Go," Jirral urged.

I spun and raced after Ina. I was being ridiculous. The old man didn't need protecting. He'd bail at the first sign of trouble, or at least not argue with the trouble when it arrived. And thus, not leaving him in charge of anyone's safety would always be the better plan.

I caught up to Ina and together, we sped across the seafloor. After a few moments, I picked up on the caves and, from the way Ina turned, I could tell she sensed them as well. The dark shapes appeared in the murk when we came closer, as did a slim crack in one of the rocky faces.

Motioning for Ina to stay put, I slipped inside. It was pitch black, so black that even my eyes had trouble with the darkness, but my senses told me the space was empty and easily large enough for us to remain hidden for a time. I returned to the opening.

"Come on," I whispered.

Ina looked around, confirming that we were alone, and then ducked through the sliver of an entrance to join me. In the darkness, she twisted slightly, reaching into her bag, and then drew something from it a moment later.

A small water-torch flared to life with blue-white light.

I glanced to the cave opening, hoping no one but Jirral would come close enough to see it.

"So, um," Ina started in a quiet voice. "About that back there. Those things that were attacking you…"

"Greliarans," I said.

"Greliarans. And they are…?"

I hesitated. "It's sort of a—"

"Long story," she finished with a nod. "Right."

She fidgeted with the torch for a moment before turning away and swimming to the cave wall, where she notched the end of the torch into a small crevice.

I tried not to grimace. "What about you?" I asked, the words coming out more irritated than I intended. "What're you doing out here? I told you to stay with Ren."

"Ren didn't believe me," she replied, not turning around. "When I told him about Niall…" She shrugged.

I couldn't stop a grimace this time. "He wouldn't listen because it came from me."

There was hardly a question in the words. There didn't need to be.

She seemed to struggle with a response. "Zeke, no. He just—"

"You're telling me that wasn't it?"

The pained expression on her face strengthened. She looked away again.

I closed my eyes. It was stupid, taking things out on Ina. It wasn't her fault. My oldest brother had always been an uptight, self-righteous jerk, and now he was king. It'd only made matters worse. And he'd despised me since we were both kids, believing I was irresponsible and a poor reflection on the monarchy. Of course he wouldn't trust anything to do with me, even when it came to something actually serious. He hadn't believed me about Chloe, after all. Hell, he'd chained her like a prisoner and left her in a pit with criminals rather than listen to me.

A quiver passed through me at the memory, and at what happened when the Sylphaen found her later.

Ren should have listened to Ina, though, no matter *who* had given her the message. He should have protected his only surviving sister, the one he'd *never* despise no matter how much she acted exactly like me.

"He's just trying to hold our family together," Ina said.

"Yeah, right," I replied before I could stop myself.

"Zeke."

I winced at the pleading note in her voice. "I'm sorry," I sighed.

She was quiet. I glanced over at her, my eyebrow lifting in emphasis.

Ina nodded.

"So then what happened?" I asked. "Why are you with Jirral?"

She hesitated. We were still on touchy ground when it came to our grandfather and she knew it. "Because seeing Niall, knowing what he'd done, what he *was*..." She seemed to struggle for words. "It didn't go well. So I found Granddad, and he *did* believe me. And you."

I didn't respond.

"He wanted me to stay with some friends in Teariad while he searched for you," she continued when her words had no effect. "But I wouldn't agree to it. I wanted to help too."

The corner of her mouth lifted in a tiny smile.

Uncomfortable, I dropped my gaze to the ground. A moment crept past.

"You were gone a long time, though."

I hesitated. I could hear the careful question in her tone, along with the hint of accusation and hurt.

And I didn't know what to say.

"Where *were* you?"

"Kansas."

Silence followed. I looked back to see her eyebrows rise.

"It's this thing," I explained, "like what Chloe does with the water. It got me there. Made the pain of the distance from the ocean go away. So I…"

I shifted my shoulders with discomfort. It'd been over a week since I left. If I'd turned back when the ocean had started hurting, the trip home would've only taken a day or so. But one thing had led to another and…

"There was this guy who came after us," I said, "and then these other guys too. Greliarans. And it just…" I trailed off. That hadn't been all of it. I didn't know what to say to Ina about the other parts. "I had to make sure Chloe was okay."

"Ah," Ina replied.

I turned my attention to the cave opening. We probably needed to stop talking. If mercenaries or soldiers came by, they could–

"I was worried," she continued. "After what happened with

Niall… with Dad."

I winced again. I'd taken off right after Dad died. Only a few hours after the physician, Liana, had killed our father, I'd left Ina in the palace.

"I'm sorry," I said.

The words weren't even close to enough. I knew that. I'd just needed to be certain Chloe was alright. She'd been a victim of all that too, and there only because I'd told her Nyciena would be safe.

I couldn't have left her to the Sylphaen and Ren. And later, when we'd been on the way to the coast, I'd tried to warn Ina. It was pathetic, really, doing nothing more than calling her in the midst of all that. But there hadn't been a choice. We'd been miles from Nyciena. Mercenaries had been everywhere. There was no way we would have made it back without Niall or the Vetorians catching us again.

And I'd figured Ren would protect our sister. I'd thought he'd at *least* be smart enough to do that.

Ina was silent. I looked back.

"Really." I swam over to her. "I am. I didn't mean to scare you, or leave for that long. Things just… they got out of control."

She hesitated, and then moved closer, letting me pull her into a hug. Her head on my shoulder, she gave a small nod.

I held her for another moment before releasing her. We both sank down, taking seats on the cave floor.

"How much longer do you think Granddad will be?" Ina

asked, her fingers tracing swirls through the sand below us.

I shrugged.

"And Chloe," she continued, still watching the sand. "Where's she heading?"

"To that guy down south, like I said."

"After that."

I hesitated. "I'm not sure."

She didn't speak for a moment. "You worried she won't come back with you?"

I blinked, my brow furrowing. "What? No, I–" I shook my head. "It'll be fine."

Ina paused. "Okay."

I glanced to her. "What?"

"Nothing."

My expression didn't change, but I looked away again.

Torchlight flickered over the cave and beyond the crack in the wall, the ocean seemed lifeless.

"You're in love with her, aren't you?" Ina said quietly. "Like… really. Not just like with the others."

Watching the cave entrance, I didn't respond. I didn't know *how* to respond. The words were… I didn't know how to wrap my head around them. I cared for Chloe. The thought of something happening to her scared me in this deep way I couldn't quite describe. I wanted the world to be safe for her, and when I was with her… when she looked at me and her smile lit up her eyes…

I drew a rough breath. I'd been with plenty of girls. Chloe

wasn't like them. I couldn't even explain how. She just wasn't. Everything about her wasn't.

And she made me want to spend the rest of my life figuring out why.

"Egan and I are back together," Ina said.

I blinked, looking over at her. It took me a moment to place the name of the guy she'd spent time with earlier in the summer. The one whose argument with her had ended me up searching for her in Santa Lucina a lifetime ago.

Ina's lip twitched. "Sometimes it's nice to have somebody in your life who wants more than just a bit of fun."

I hesitated and then nodded, slowly mirroring the smile. "Yeah."

Her grin spread and she rocked over, nudging my shoulder. "Don't worry. I saw her when we were leaving the beach. I'm pretty sure she's crazy about you too."

I kept smiling, trying to look convinced even if I wasn't so sure. There was still that other guy in her life. There were still all sorts of dangers out here.

Chloe had a ton of reasons to get as far from the ocean as possible.

And not that many to stay.

A rock skittered down near the entrance of the cave. I started up from the ground as Ina's breath caught. Quickly, she darted over to the torch and grabbed it from the crevice.

She plunged the blue-white flame into the sand. The cave went black. Cautiously, I swam toward the opening in the stone wall.

"Ina?" Jirral whispered. "Zeke?"

A small sound escaped Ina. "Granddad?"

I felt someone slide through the crack of the cave. By the opposite wall, the torch flared back to life.

Jirral blinked in the light, the blue glow of his eyes fading to a fraction of its brightness.

"Is everything alright?" Ina asked.

"A couple mercenaries poking around the area," he answered. "There are hills ahead, though, and they didn't seem too interested in searching them." He paused. "We should probably circle wide, just in case they have friends hiding there."

I grimaced. That would slow us down.

A lot.

"Chloe is going to be there in just a few hours," I said.

"And getting caught by Vetorians will take a great deal longer than a small detour," Jirral countered.

I looked away, hating the fact he was right. I didn't want to miss her, though. If that Joseph guy did his thing, and if she became a landwalker and had to leave the coast right away…

"We'll be fast," Jirral added, his tone a touch gentler.

I nodded tightly.

"Alright," Jirral said. "Follow me."

15

WYATT

I shoved to my feet, the last of the sticky, elastic vine things snapping away from my body.

But the fish were gone.

An infuriated snarl left me while I scanned the yard. They were gone. All of them were gone, from the girl and the black-haired guy to Niall and his cronies.

And I hadn't gotten my hands on a single one.

Not. A. *Single. One.*

My body shook. I wanted to make something bleed. I wanted to hear something scream. It wouldn't be as good as killing a scum-sucker but damn it all, it'd be *something*.

Dad growled as he ripped the vines away and pushed to his feet behind me. Far down the road from our house, I could hear sirens, like a whispering wail across the distance.

"Free your brothers," Dad ordered me.

I didn't move. "What are we going to do now?"

"Cops are coming."

I waited. He wasn't even looking at me. "And?"

"And we've got dead bodies in the yard!" Dad snapped, turning a glare on me. "Cops are a problem, Wyatt. Cops are *always* a problem, whether we have a deal with the landwalkers or not, so fucking hurry up, get your brothers free, and clear that crap out of sight!"

With a disgusted noise, he stalked away, shaking his head like he couldn't believe me.

My brow rose. We were backing down? Staying put? *Cleaning up?* After all the days of waiting, after all the hours of being surrounded by scale-skins he said we couldn't lay a *finger* on, Dad seriously expected us to just give up and go back to the drawing board?

"But we could catch her," I tried. "If we go now…"

Dad ignored me.

I stared, appalled. This wasn't happening. I'd done everything he wanted, followed stupid plan after stupid plan, and I didn't have a single thing to show for it. Clay did. That mewling bastard had lost it in the forest just like I'd known he would, but he'd still gotten to kill *two* of the scum-suckers with his bare hands.

But I had nothing. Absolutely nothing.

Dad stopped by the corner of the house. With one arm, he braced himself on the siding, his gaze on the ocean like he could see that Zeke guy in the water.

Nothing.

Rage surged through me and my feet were moving before I

registered the impulse. Fire sped beneath my skin, bursting out through fissures.

Dad heard me coming. He started to turn.

I lunged through the air and collided with him hard. The impact drove him into the wall and slammed his head into the siding. He staggered, his skin changing fast.

But it was too late.

My hands twisted. His neck snapped in my grasp.

I stumbled back as he fell, his body collapsing like the dead weight that it was. My heart raced in my ears and my breathing came in quick, ragged gasps. I couldn't take my eyes from him. Dad. Dead on the ground.

A shiver coursed through me. My lips curled into an unsteady smile. I'd done it. I'd *actually* done it.

I'd won.

Clay made a sound and my gaze darted toward him. Still trapped under the vines, he struggled to break free, while a few yards away, Owen tried to do the same. Their motions were weak, as if between killing those dehaians and fighting to escape the vines, they were exhausted.

But behind the gaps in the nets covering them, their eyes were locked on me.

My smile grew cold. I walked toward Clay.

He struggled harder, but only a couple vines broke. I stopped when I reached him, and for a moment, I just studied him.

"You got a problem with this?" I asked, my voice low.

He paused. "No."

My lip twitched. "Good."

I left him there while I crossed the yard to Owen. Clay was younger and thus potentially less of a threat, but he'd also gotten to kill dehaians and he'd always been more of a pain in the ass than Owen. It was important to make his place clear fast. Grasping the vines pinning Owen down, I ripped them free. He pushed to his feet.

His gaze went to Dad. Eyeing Owen, I waited for him to make a move.

Old anger twitched across his face, along with a heavy dose of contempt. "Bastard," he muttered. He looked back to me, and his chin jerked in implicit congratulations.

I nodded. Owen walked over and tugged the vines from Clay.

"We're going after the girl," I said. "Get the car."

"What about the bodies?" Clay asked.

I glanced to Dad. The cops would be here any second. We didn't have long to reach the side road out of here.

And besides that, I didn't care.

I scoffed and started toward the maroon SUV. "Let 'em rot."

16

CHLOE

We barely made it to the main road before Olivia slowed the car again.

And a chilling wave of suspicion stole over me when I saw why.

A dozen vehicles were parked along the grassy roadside, with several police cars as well. Cops were there, surveying the forest or talking with a cluster of people nearby.

But I'd never seen such a motley group. Not outside of a Hollywood rendition of a jury, anyway. Business men stood next to guys who appeared to have just come from construction sites, while women who looked like politicians were speaking to others who seemed like soccer moms. More people were beyond them, leaning on the vehicles as if they could barely stay on their feet. Past the fringes of the group, Ellie waited with Baylie by her car, and both of them were watching the small crowd warily.

"Olivia…" I began, "who are these people?"

"The elders decided to meet us here," she replied.

"Excuse me?" Noah demanded from the back seat. "You *do* realize my family will be coming, right? We don't have time for this."

Olivia pulled the car over and then pushed the gearshift into park. "We'll only be a moment," she countered calmly. "The elders have the right to speak with her, and they were willing to endure the pain from their proximity to the water to do so. After all, this could be their only chance."

"Wait, why?" Mom interjected, scooting forward. "Chloe, what does that mean?"

Olivia ignored her. "They simply want to talk," she said to me. "Please allow them that."

My brow drew down. I twisted in the seat, looking to Noah.

"What is there to talk about?" he asked warily.

Olivia's gaze didn't leave me. "Please."

"Chloe," Dad protested. "No. We're heading home, understand?"

I swallowed. That wasn't going to happen.

But this wasn't good either.

"Ma'am," Dad continued to Olivia. "I appreciate you driving us, and helping us escape those creatures, but we need to take our daughter home. This craziness has to end."

Olivia ignored him just like she had Mom. "Ten minutes. Then we'll go."

She turned and left the car.

I glanced to Noah. Caution clear on his face, he opened his

door as well.

Dad made an angry noise. "Chloe, don't–"

I followed Noah.

One of the elders motioned the rest into silence when we stepped from the sedan. By the side of the road, more elders straightened, bracing themselves on their vehicles to keep their balance. Catching sight of us, Baylie pushed away from her car and hurried toward us, Ellie on her heels.

"Are you okay?" Baylie called.

Sweat dripping down his red face, Phil shoved past the group. "Is she here? Are they– Olivia!" He turned to the police. "Go! Make sure those guys don't try following."

The cops didn't even question him. Without a word, they climbed back into their cars.

I stared, creeped out by how much authority the elders obviously had.

"What took so long?" Phil continued, ignoring the police while they drove away.

"Oh, give Olivia a break, Phil," Robin admonished, following after him. I could see her shaking, though she seemed to be doing a bit better than the others. "She was dealing with greliarans. It'd take a bit to convince those creatures to see sense and back down."

Olivia didn't contradict the statement. From the corner of my eye, I saw Noah scowl.

"Is everything alright?" Ellie asked. "Did they–" She glanced around. "Where's Zeke?"

I hesitated.

"His family showed up," Noah explained. "They're going to meet us."

Ellie's brow rose. "More dehaians?"

"Is he alright?" Baylie asked, watching me.

I nodded.

"You should have brought them here too," Phil told Olivia. "They could have–"

"How would they fit them in the car?" Robin interrupted. "Honestly, Phil, sometimes you're just so–"

"I only meant that we could have talked to–"

"Enough," Olivia cut in before they could continue arguing. She glanced to me. "If you'd come this way?"

Warily, I followed her. Noah stayed close, watching the others as if daring them to try anything. The elders stared while we walked over, and I couldn't help but notice they weren't looking at anyone but me.

"So," Olivia said, seeming unfazed by the silent observation. "Everyone, this is Chloe Kowalski. As you've undoubtedly already noticed from Dave and Ellie's lack of reaction to the ocean, what I described to Robin on the phone is true. Chloe can affect the magic created by our ancestors."

"Will she help us?" a man in paint-stained overalls asked.

Noah muttered a curse. "I knew it. You're not using her to–"

"We haven't discussed the agreement yet," Olivia interrupted, regarding Noah and the other man equally. She turned to me. "Chloe, as I said, the elders simply wish to speak with you. We still support you continuing with our plan for you to visit Joseph, and we recognize that *choice* may not be involved in whichever side of your heritage you fully become. But we would ask that, should you have the option, you remain on land among our people."

"What is this?" Dad asked. "Chloe, what are they talking–"

"She's going to become landwalker or dehaian, Mr. Kowalski," Olivia said. "Not both."

His brow rose. My stomach churned at the hope in his eyes.

"But that brings me to the reason we're here," Olivia continued. "We would like to make an arrangement."

Noah scoffed. "Oh, great. Yeah, you're good at those."

I glanced to him, silently agreeing.

Olivia appeared unfazed by the comment. "We would like to offer you the opportunity to become an elder."

I blinked.

Behind me, Mom made a choked noise. "What? Really? Oh, Chloe!"

Her hands grabbed my shoulders. I jumped, barely keeping spikes from coming out of my arms.

"This… oh my gracious," Mom sputtered. "Chloe, you could–"

"In exchange," Olivia continued over her. "We would ask that you use what you can do to give the elders freedom from the pain of the ocean."

"That seems fair," Mom agreed. "I don't see why Chloe couldn't–"

I pulled away from her, taking a step closer to the elders just to put distance between us.

"Chloe?" Mom tried.

I stared between them all. There was no way in hell I was staying a landwalker. Not if I had a choice. And now these crazy elder people wanted me to… to what? Magic them into being able to remain here, when the effects probably wouldn't even last a day?

"Why?" I asked, incredulous.

"Honey, you can't question an eld–"

"Yes, I can!" I snapped at Mom.

She stopped, startled.

"*Why?*" I repeated. "It won't last. It'll be gone the minute he splits this… this whatever I am. And if the Beast feels it…"

I shook my head at Olivia, unable to wrap my head around what they were thinking.

"Do you *want* that thing to pick up on her?" Noah added in a dangerous tone.

I glanced to him. Looking cautious as hell, he was eyeing the others. From the tension on his face, I could tell he was barely keeping himself from changing.

"No," Olivia replied. "Of course we don't. We would merely like the opportunity to study the ocean, our proximity to it, and the differences between our current state and what you can provide. And there is the possibility, however remote, that what you do will remain even after Joseph completes the procedure." She paused. "Chloe, I realize you've had trouble trusting us –

me – and I understand why. But please, try to trust me now. This is our only chance. As it stands, the medicines they've taken to reach this place will hospitalize the elders in not too much longer if you don't help them. They knew that. They came anyway. That is how important this is to us. There isn't anyone capable of pushing back the ocean's pain as you do, and once you become like us or the modern-day dehaians, that ability will almost certainly be gone."

I looked to the elders. Some of them were back to leaning on their vehicles, their eyes closed and their faces tight, while others had sunk to the ground, trembling. I hated the sight of it. I couldn't believe they'd put themselves through this. Last chance or not, they seemed like they were dying, and some part of me wanted to go over there right now, just to stop what obviously was agony to them.

And yet…

"Now, to be fair," Olivia added, "I must warn you that becoming an elder would not necessarily be a guarantee. It would require testing."

I turned back to her sharply.

"Not like what you've experienced, however," she assured me quickly. "Simply aptitude tests to determine if you are capable of developing our specific skill set. All elder potentiates go through them."

She glanced to Ellie, an expectant look on her face.

The girl gave a small nod. "It's fine. Just pictures and mental exercises and stuff."

I didn't respond. Ellie sounded edgy, and miserable as well, and she seemed like she wanted to be anywhere but on this road with the elders all around.

Olivia paused, regarding the girl for a moment, and then continued as if attempting to ignore the tone. "With the abilities you've shown already," she said to me, "I have no doubt you will pass. So, Chloe, do we have an agreement?"

I stared at them. Each elder still standing watched me, and they barely seemed to breathe. Hope showed in the eyes of most of them, while in a few others, the expression was mixed with a weird sort of envy.

They wanted this. They wanted this as badly as Ellie had wanted to become dehaian. It wasn't any different. Not really. They'd given up being dehaian, but they hadn't stopped wanting to come here.

And I could understand that. Good grief, I could understand that.

My gaze slid to Olivia. But it still didn't mean they were trustworthy. Not by a long shot. It didn't mean something else wasn't going on.

I glanced to Ellie. Her expression hadn't changed.

"Can I talk to you?" I murmured to her.

She blinked. With a quick glance from me to the elders, she nodded. I retreated toward Baylie's car. Ellie hurried after me, Baylie coming a step behind.

My parents tried to follow. A warning sound from Noah brought them up short.

"What is it?" I asked softly. "What's with the look?"

Ellie hesitated, her gaze flicking to the others. Several yards away, my parents hovered as close as they dared to Noah, who had taken up a position as a buffer between us and everyone else on the road. The elders still watched us, though they glanced to their friends with every few heartbeats as if fighting the urge to speak to each other.

I realized they probably knew what Noah was, through Dave telling them if nothing else.

"They're probably okay," Ellie said.

I turned back to her.

She looked uncomfortable. "It's just what that cop claimed. I know Olivia said the ones that 'sided' with Grandpa or whatever would be kept out of the loop, but…" She grimaced. "Grandpa has a *lot* of friends, and I… I don't want to speak badly of the elders. I mean, they'd know about this more than me, and I'm not a–"

"Just say it," Baylie snapped.

Ellie winced. "What if someone is lying? What if they agree with Grandpa, but they just haven't said anything to make Olivia think they're not on her side? I really don't want the elders to be in pain, but if you give them this ability, it *doesn't* go away after this procedure thing, and then they're like him…"

My skin crawled.

"I don't want anyone hurting people like he did either," Ellie finished.

"She's right," Baylie said quietly. "You can't risk it. I mean,

Harman took a *knife* to Zeke, for pity's sake. And I saw Zeke's arms. What that guy did to those spike things of his. If people like that could come here whenever they wanted…"

I nodded tightly. If even *one* of them was the same as Harman and they got their hands on a dehaian…

I shuddered. Ina liked to come inland. Surely other dehaians did too. And then there were kids. Maybe someone Zeke's little sister's age, who'd die like Miri had, but with that bastard or one of his friends experimenting on her…

My throat clenched with nausea. Drawing a ragged breath, I shoved the thoughts away. "Yeah," I agreed.

Baylie glanced to the elders. "So how do we–"

Tires rumbled on the road. I turned. A trio of sedans rolled to a stop, all three of them painted in subdued shades of taupe with the look of undercover police vehicles.

My brow drew down. How many cops did the elders control?

The doors opened. A tiny gasp escaped me, the sound incredulous.

This couldn't be happening.

"Hey there, folks," Chief Reynolds called, his voice strained to a fraction of its normal friendliness. From the other cars, the men from Colorado emerged, some of them barely making it to their feet before they had to brace themselves on the sedans for support. Aaron joined them, trembling hard with his gaze twitching between me and the elders like he couldn't decide who worried him more.

Harman climbed from the passenger seat of Chief Reynolds'

sedan.

I wanted to turn and run.

"There she is," Harman said, motioning to the men by the cars and then pointing at me. He didn't even glance at the elders. "The dehaian boy should be somewhere close as well."

"What are you doing here?" Olivia demanded, moving between us and Harman's people.

Robin followed her, as did several of the others who could still walk. Keeping his eyes to the men around the taupe cars, Noah closed the distance between us. I could see hair-thin lines of light running through his skin.

"Olivia," Harman called cheerily, seeming unaffected by the ocean's proximity. "Everyone. What a pleasure to see you. I'm here to collect the young lady."

"The hell you are!" Olivia snapped. "How did you know we would–"

"I have friends, of course," he interrupted as though it was obvious. "They're just as invested in my research and the girl's wellbeing as I am."

Olivia glanced around, incredulity in her eyes. I swallowed hard, doing the same. I could read the implication. Ellie had been right.

"Mr. and Mrs. Kowalski," Harman continued, spotting Mom and Dad. "How nice to see you as well."

"You…" Dad snarled, stalking forward. "You *bastard*! Your 'assistants' nearly *killed* us! What were you–"

"I promise you," Harman said as the chief stepped in front

of him, bringing Dad's advance to a halt. "I had no idea they would do that. I had no idea what they *were*. I only pieced the truth together myself a few minutes ago, based on what I heard through the police scanner. I am *terribly* sorry. It was my understanding that my associates were, well, just healthy land-walkers. And only interested in recovering the girl to *help* her."

Dad didn't respond.

"I swear," Harman insisted. "Now, please. Allow us to bring your daughter inland. I believe this much exposure to the ocean air will set us back on treating her condition, so it's important we leave as soon as possible."

His gaze turned to me and shivers ran through my skin. It was like he didn't care how many people were between us. Like he didn't even see them.

"You're not going *near* her!" Olivia snapped. "You–"

"We can help your daughter, Mr. Kowalski," Harman said, ignoring her. "I don't want to think of the damage more time away from the treatments could–"

"Stop it!"

I blinked at Ellie's outburst.

Her curly braids trembling, she stared at him. "Stop *lying*, Grandpa! Your 'treatments' almost *killed* Chloe! You–"

"Oh, Eleanor," Harman commented as though just noticing the girl. He looked to Dad. "My granddaughter is correct, in the latter part at least. The treatments *did* almost kill Chloe, but because Eleanor took it upon herself to remove your daughter from our care."

Ellie gasped. "That's not–"

"I forgive you, my dear," Harman continued blithely, "and I'm sure the Kowalskis will too. I realize you didn't understand that your actions could have cost Chloe her life."

Hurt and outrage in her eyes, Ellie shook her head. "That is *not true*! You *were* killing her! *And* Zeke! He almost–"

"Nonsense," Harman countered. "Dehaians don't feel pain as we do. Everyone knows that, and my experiments proved it. The boy barely cried out. He was fine."

Spikes pushed out of my arms. I couldn't stop them. To hear him talk so calmly about *torturing* Zeke…

Harman caught sight of them, and he made a pitying noise. "Don't worry, dear. Those will be gone soon."

He motioned for the men around him to move toward us.

Olivia retreated a step, keeping herself between them and us. "You are *not* doing this, Harman. If I have to, I–"

The cocking of a gun cut her off. She looked over in alarm.

"I wouldn't," Phil cautioned, a handgun in his meaty grip.

Olivia stared at him. "You…"

"I told you we should have just put the girl underground," he continued. "We could've avoided all of this and made her much easier for Harman to find."

Robin stumbled forward, her face pale. "Phil, you *idiot*! You can't let him just *experiment* on her! What about the–"

"A few storms don't make an apocalypse, Robin," Phil replied tiredly.

She blinked, incredulous. "Don't you get it? This is *wrong*!

You can't–"

Robin cut off when he pointed the gun toward her.

Olivia tensed.

Phil gasped. He looked to Olivia furiously, his face twitching as if he was fighting something no one else could see.

"No…" he snarled.

His gun swung toward her so fast.

The shot rang through the forest.

Olivia choked. Staggering back, she lost her balance and fell to her knees. Her hand clutched her shoulder, pain written across her face.

"Bastard!" Robin cried. She rushed to Olivia. Noah grabbed Ellie's arm, stopping her from doing the same.

"I can patch that up for you," Harman told Olivia. "No worries." He turned his gaze to us. "Now please, everyone. Allow Chloe to come with me."

Chief Reynolds and the men with him drew their guns. Behind him, Aaron hesitated, and then cautiously did the same.

Phil aimed his weapon toward the rest of the elders. "All of you stay there. We just want the girl."

He started toward us.

Fissures bright with firelight raced through Noah's skin.

Dad moved into Phil's path. "You can't–"

Phil shoved him hard, sending him staggering to the side, and then he lifted the gun, aiming at Noah.

"Back off, kid," Phil warned.

Noah strode toward him.

A glowing blur slammed into Phil, driving the gun from his hands and propelling him sideways into the trees. Another greliaran hit two of the men beside Chief Reynolds, throwing them both back into a sedan.

Snarling, Clay spun. His burning gaze went from me to Noah for less than a heartbeat, and then he lunged.

Noah intercepted him. They both tumbled to the gravel.

Gunshots rang through the forest. I looked up fast.

The men around Harman had scattered. In a panic, they fired at Owen as he charged them. In the center of the road, Dave scrambled to help Robin and Olivia while the other elders fled for their own vehicles. The elders surrounded Mom and Dad, jostling them when they ran past. I saw Mom fall.

A laugh came from my right. I turned.

Wyatt grinned, fiery cracks spreading through his face and his brown eyes disappearing into a red glow.

"Chloe, run!" my dad yelled.

Wyatt raced at me. I backpedaled, with Baylie and Ellie retreating behind me.

Noah slammed into him, driving him to the ground. Several feet away, Clay rolled to one side, shaking his head as if to clear it.

Ellie grabbed Baylie and me, pulling us with her. "Come on!"

We ran for the car.

"Noah!" Baylie yelled.

He shoved away from Wyatt and raced after us.

I yanked open the rear door and scrambled inside while Baylie jammed the key into the ignition. I spun, looking through the back window.

The elders' vehicles were tearing pell-mell down the country road. Dave and Robin were bundling Olivia into the woman's sedan and motioning for my parents to come with them.

And Wyatt was getting up. Behind him, Clay was pushing to his feet as well. Under fire from the rest of Chief Reynolds' men, Owen was retreating into the forest while Harman ignored them all, shouting and waving at us as though to signal the others that we were getting away.

Noah tumbled into the seat beside me.

Baylie hit the gas.

The car surged forward, leaving the chaos behind.

17

WYATT

By all that was holy, that was going to be the last time Noah and his damn stepsister drove off with my fish.

The *absolute* last.

I turned away while the stepsister's car whipped around the curve and disappeared. Back by the junction of the road to our house, the elders were taking off like the hounds of hell were on their tail. Narrowly avoiding getting hit when the cars sped away, the big guys with guns bundled Harman into one of their brown sedans, ignoring his cries about the girl escaping.

"Hey, wait!" Clay shouted, running toward them. "Where are they going? Where's the girl–"

Cars doors slammed. Gravel sprayed as the brown sedans raced off.

And then no one remained but us.

Snarling a curse, I looked around at the empty forest. That *couldn't* be it. They were gone, *she* was gone, and we'd lost her trail. I wanted to run to the SUV right now, except that we'd left it a quarter mile back and by the time I made it there, she'd be even farther away. There were half a dozen paths out of here down that road; she could take any one.

But there had to be something else we could do. Somewhere else we could follow her. Harman wanted to get his hands on the fish too. Maybe we could call the little bastard.

I snorted at the thought. This wasn't like Dad's strategy. I wasn't above calling people, but I also wasn't going to sit around waiting for her to come to me. I'd take action. I'd chase her down.

And then I'd make her pay for getting away from me over and over again.

I started back down the road. It'd been a good plan, all things considered. Everything had been going great. We'd driven along the side road and the cops hadn't even noticed us as they'd flown by on the main path. We'd kept the windows down, listening for any signs of others nearby, and soon enough picked up the sounds of an argument. The idiots had stopped along the road like they didn't even think we'd be coming, and not a single one had noticed when we'd pulled over and then snuck through the forest toward them.

Of course, moving through the forest in silence was sort of our specialty. Catching dehaians who wandered onto our property would require not barreling toward them like a herd of cattle, after all. Dad had made a point of teaching us to move fast and quiet, and forced us to practice till even he couldn't hear us coming.

Not smart, that.

My lip twitched. But regardless, things had been going well. We'd seen the landwalkers, the girl's parents, all of them.

And the fish.

She'd been so close. Just beyond the trees, without Noah or any of those damn elders nearby. I'd sent Clay at Noah and Owen toward the big guys with guns, which left me that pretty little doll of a black girl and the stepsister all alone with my fish.

And it should have worked. It *all* should have worked.

If Clay had stopped Noah like he'd been supposed to, anyway.

Still rubbing his jaw from the punch Noah had landed on him, Clay watched me while I stalked toward him.

"So what are we going to–"

I slammed a fist into his face.

"Dumbass," I spat as he stumbled back. "How could you let him get away from you like that?"

"He got away from you too," Clay protested.

I growled. He retreated a step.

"Hey," Owen called. "We got a live one over here."

I turned. By the intersection, Owen hoisted himself up the last step of the incline leading from the forest to the road. Leaving Clay, I strode toward him.

"There," he said, nodding toward the underbrush.

A man lay in the ditch below him. Dressed in a navy sports jacket with brass buttons that strained to hold the thing closed over his bulk, he was slumped against a tree with blood dripping from a gash on his bald head.

"Help…" he wheezed, his eyes closed. "Somebody help…"

"Clay ran into him," Owen murmured, watching the guy. "He had a gun."

I glanced to the man's hands. "Not anymore."

Skidding on the grass, I climbed down to where the man lay.

His hand fumbled toward me. "Please. Please, help…"

"Yeah," I agreed, moving my foot out of his reach. "Sure, we'll help you. Don't worry. Just tell us, though. Where's the girl headed?"

"Girl?" He opened his eyes with effort. "But– oh God. You–"

The fear on his face made me smile. I crouched down and watched him try to scoot away, not that the attempt worked. He could barely move.

"Simple deal, buddy," I said. "You want help. We want the girl. Where is she?"

He seemed to be having trouble breathing and for a heartbeat, he almost appeared to debate answering. I started to stand again.

"Okay," the guy relented. "They're heading south. She's… it's…"

I reached down, grasping his sports jacket. "Where?"

He mumbled a string of numbers. My brow furrowed in confusion.

"Latitude and longitude," Owen said behind me.

I didn't turn around. "I knew that."

"Now, please," the man begged. "Please call the–"

I shoved him back into the tree again. His neck broke on the impact.

A faint, tingling sensation rushed along my arm, through my chest and up to my head, almost like adrenaline coming from outside me. But better than that. *So* much better. My lip spasmed toward a snarl, my brain torn between pleasure and shock.

As fast as it'd appeared, the feeling faded away.

I stared down at the guy's corpse. Dad had warned us about the landwalker elders. Told us to stay away from them. They were dangerous, he said.

He'd never mentioned this.

It wasn't like the stories. The shiver of magic that'd left the guy wasn't anything like the overpowering high that came from a fish's death. I'd seen the strength of that on Clay's face when he'd taken down those two dehaians back by the house. This didn't even come close.

But it was something. The landwalkers had something.

And it'd felt pretty damn amazing, even if only for a heartbeat.

No wonder they wanted us living on the coast away from them.

I drew a breath. I wouldn't let Owen or Clay know. Compared to Clay's dead scale-skins, this was nothing, and I didn't want to be the brother who got the substitute kills. I was in charge and I was still going to be the one to get the girl.

And besides, information was power. I wasn't sure how this bit would help me, but that wasn't important right now.

I straightened again and turned back to Owen. "Get the car. We've got a fish to catch."

18

ZEKE

Circling the hills to reach Chloe couldn't have taken longer if we'd been swimming through concrete.

Fighting back impatience, I cast another look to Jirral while we swam through the twilight deep. We'd been giving wide berth to the hills where he thought mercenaries might be hiding, and out of self-preservation, we'd barely said a word in that time. All my attempts to go faster had been met with glares from Jirral, though. The fact he was in better shape than many dehaians half his age wasn't the point. I'd won more than my fair share of races back home and had adrenaline working for me besides. Ina would stay with me – she was lightning fast when she wanted to be – but that meant nothing for him. He wouldn't stand a chance of keeping up if we pushed any harder than we already were.

I was just having trouble caring. Not with the minutes ticking away.

The ocean floor started to drop lower beneath us and Jirral motioned for us to turn, a signal that the hills far to our left had finally ended. Cutting sharply toward the distant shore, I started swimming faster.

Jirral made an irritated noise.

I kept going. I knew it would take Chloe several hours to travel there, and I figured it'd take that Joseph guy some time beyond that to get things ready to change her in the way our ancestors had apparently done. But it didn't matter. I wouldn't leave her a second longer than I had to in all this.

A half dozen shapes appeared in the distance ahead, racing toward us.

I pulled up fast while behind me, Jirral muttered a curse. Quickly, we spun, taking off in the opposite direction.

There were six more in the water that way.

Turning hard, we sped south.

Three others were there, lost in the murk and heading toward us.

"What the–" Ina gasped.

"Hills," Jirral ordered.

We swam, water rushing around us while the shapes in the distance came closer.

Another group rose from the invisible hills, their forms strange in the water. Ina made a desperate noise.

"Come on," Jirral snapped.

We dove, following him while he tried to cut a path under the ones to the east. I wasn't sure it would work; we were so deep already, the space beneath them was limited. But they were spread out toward the surface and coming at us from every side.

There weren't many options left.

We veered away from the seafloor and kept going. The dehaians turned, plummeting toward us. Jirral fought to keep up while Ina and I darted beneath them.

Small shapes sped through the water like torpedoes.

Jirral shouted furiously.

I spun. Nets encased him. Yanking the knife from her belt, Ina raced back to his side. Grabbing the vines, she worked frantically to free him.

And then the dehaians were on us.

A guy slammed into me, sending us both spinning through the water. His arm wrapped around my throat while his other hand grabbed for my wrist, attempting to pin it behind my back. Another dehaian rushed toward me, a net-gun in his hands.

I drove an elbow into the midsection of the one holding me and then twisted in his grip, my spikes slashing across his ribs.

His hold broke. Blood filled the water.

I darted to the side and pods shot through the water where I'd been, striking the bleeding man behind me. Kicking hard, I took off for Ina. Nets still clung to Jirral. At his side, Ina was working to free him while slashing at the speeding forms of the attackers to keep them from coming near.

"Leave me, girl!" Jirral yelled. "Get out of here!"

Two more dehaians charged at me, while another rushed down from above. I jack-knifed in the water, trying to get out of their way.

Nets came at me from three sides.

I twisted, but it was too late.

Vines raced over me and then the guys were there. A fist slammed into my face, snapping my head to the side. Another plowed hard into my stomach. Tentacles pinned my arms awkwardly, making it impossible to fight back, while others climbed over my head and face, obscuring my view.

"Stop!" a man shouted.

The dehaians froze.

I struggled in the nets. Through the tangle of vines, I caught sight of more dehaians circling us. They had Ina surrounded. There were knives in their hands. I ripped at the tentacles holding me, desperate to reach her.

One of the dehaians punched me hard in the side.

"I said stop!"

Choking, I looked up. A trio of dehaians were approaching.

I recognized the bronze-scaled, dark-haired one at the center. Tiberion. One of Ren's commanders. A black band wrapped his bicep now, the fabric stitched with metallic thread in the shape of a mountain that was underlined in stars, marking him as the captain of the guard. Other people followed him, pulling blindfolded and bound dehaians in their wake.

My gaze flicked over the prisoners. Empty sheaths for knives were strapped to their scarred chests. Welts showed on their fins where blades had been attached, the weapons now missing.

Vetorians. We'd stumbled on Ren's people while they were capturing a group of mercenaries.

"Your highness?" Tiberion said to Ina. He glanced to us, and I could see suspicion creep into his gaze when he recognized Jirral.

"Free that one," Tiberion ordered shortly, nodding toward me.

"Sir," the dehaian next to me said. "He injured Leif."

Tiberion ignored him.

The net around me loosened as the dehaians' knives sliced through it. Tentacles pulled at my skin when the guards yanked the vines covering my face away.

Spikes appeared at my throat the moment the net disappeared.

Cold fury filled Tiberion's eyes. "Prince Zekerian."

The guards glanced to each other, their expressions making clear they hadn't realized whom they'd captured.

"Tell his highness what we've found," Tiberion ordered the soldier beside him.

The man darted away.

Tiberion swam closer, looking between me and Jirral. "You *were* working with Vetorian spies, just as the king said."

I struggled in the grip of the two dehaians holding me – attempting not to cut my own throat in the process. Ina was surrounded, but the others had pulled away from her. Fear on her face, she watched me.

"We're not with them," I growled at Tiberion.

"Yes, I'm certain Princess Inasaria is not," he agreed. "You and Lord Jirral, on the other hand…" His expression made his opinion clear. "Where is the female spy? The redheaded girl who conspired to kill King Torvias?"

I didn't respond.

"Rest assured, highness," he said. "We *will* find her. The king has ordered her to stand trial and, upon proof of her guilt to the court, she is to be publicly executed for her crimes. We will see those commands carried out. Your silence gains nothing."

I stared at him. "*What?*"

"You heard him."

My gaze snapped to the water beyond Tiberion.

Niall swam up, a pair of dehaians from the attack at the greliarans' house behind him.

"Highness," Tiberion acknowledged.

"She's not here?" Niall asked shortly, studying the Vetorians chained behind Tiberion's men.

"No, sire. And the prince refuses to provide her location."

"Niall, you damned fool," Jirral snapped. "What the hell are you—"

Jirral cut off as a guard aimed a knife at his throat.

Niall ignored them, studying me, and shivers ran through me at the cold, alien expression on his face. Till a few days before, I'd never seen anything like it from him in my life.

He turned away, scanning the open water as if searching for Chloe despite Tiberion's words. My gaze darted to Ina. If Niall was here, there was no telling how many Sylphaen were also. And I didn't want my sister near them. Anywhere within a thousand miles of them. Niall had sworn not to hurt her, and coming from the brother I thought I'd known, I would have trusted that implicitly.

But I didn't even recognize the guy in front of us now.

Ina's wide eyes met mine. Heart pounding, I twitched my gaze toward the south. The fear in her expression strengthened in response. She shook her head slightly. I tensed, my own expression becoming demanding.

"Take them back to the palace," Niall ordered with a sigh. "We'll continue searching."

Tiberion glanced to his soldiers. "Chain Prince Zekerian. Lord Jirral too. We will escort them back with the others for the king's judgment."

"Niall, stop this!" Ina shouted at him. "Please!"

No one looked at her. The guards' grips tightened on me and I felt the spikes nick the skin of my neck. I couldn't move. Not without running into the blades at my throat. Another dehaian appeared in front of me.

Shackles clamped around my wrists. The spikes at my neck didn't budge.

I glanced to Jirral. Five dehaians surrounded him, all with knives drawn, and as I watched, the soldiers closed in with shackles in hand.

"Bring the princess," Tiberion ordered.

The guards started for her too. Tensing, she aimed her spikes at the dehaians coming toward her. They paused.

"Highness," Tiberion said to her. "Please. No one will harm you. We only wish to take you safely home to your brother the king."

"That's my brother too, you ass," she snapped, slashing her knife at one of the soldiers when they tried to come near. "The one in chains. Get your people away from him."

Tiberion's mouth tightened. He glanced to the guards holding me. The spikes disappeared from my throat, but from the pocket of his vest, one of them drew out a blindfold.

"Hey!" Ina protested.

I twisted, trying to keep them from putting the hood on me while I glared at my sister.

A pained look flashed across Ina's face.

Niall spotted it. "Guards, stop–"

Ina spun, taking off between two of the soldiers.

The men grabbed for her, and blood filled the water when her spikes sliced their arms. Shouting with pain, they faltered while the others around them darted away, trying to catch her.

They didn't stand a chance in hell.

Through the bloodied water, I felt her disappear from my senses as she raced south. The guards sped after her, but before they even reached the edge of what I could feel in the water, it was clear they were slowing, unable to keep up. Closer by, several others went to the aid of those she'd cut, attempting to staunch the bleeding of deep wounds that would probably attract any shark for miles around.

Niall swam toward me, ignoring them. "Smart," he commented quietly. "Sending our sister out into the ocean all alone at a time like this. Ren's sure to be sympathetic about that."

"Keeps her away from you," I retorted just as softly.

Niall paused. "I'm not the threat here, Zeke. None of us are. Sooner or later, you'll see that. But until then, rest assured, we *will* find them. Wherever they hide, we'll find them. Ina and Chloe both."

He glanced to the man beside me.

The guard pulled the hood over my head.

19

NOAH

"Okay, thank you."

Ellie hung up the phone and looked back at us.

"That was Robin," she said to Chloe. "Your mom and dad are fine. They're with her and Dave. Once they reach a hospital, she's going to stay with Olivia, but Dave and your parents will come to meet us."

In the seat next to me, Chloe nodded, her gaze lost somewhere between the back of the chair in front of her and the crossroads we'd long since left behind.

"Is Olivia alright?" Baylie asked.

"I think so," Ellie replied. "They just need to get her to a doctor."

I glanced to her, hearing the uncertainty in her voice.

"Robin told me she'd call if there was any change," Ellie finished.

Baylie made a noise of acknowledgement, her hands flexing around the steering wheel.

Silence fell over the car.

I leaned a bit closer to Chloe. "You okay?" I asked, keeping my voice low.

She hesitated, her gaze not quite turning to me. "I want this fixed. Gone."

"This isn't your fault."

She nodded, though she didn't look convinced.

I reached over, taking her hand.

She tensed and closed her eyes, her face tightening. "Please, Noah, I… "

Fighting back a grimace, I let my hand fall away. I turned to the window, while up front, Baylie and Ellie carefully gave no sign of noticing anything.

"I'm sorry," Chloe said.

I glanced back at her.

"I…" She shook her head, as though pushing a thought aside. "Are you okay? From earlier, I mean."

"Yeah."

Her brow twitched down. She still wasn't looking at me. "They were really–"

"Things don't hurt the same when we're like that."

"Oh."

I waited, but nothing else came. Exhaling, I turned back to the window. I wanted to push for more. To know what she really felt for me now, whether there was a chance in hell for us at all anymore, and what she planned to choose if she got to decide which side of her heritage she'd become. But Baylie and

Ellie were in the front, every word I said would get overheard, and Chloe obviously didn't want to talk anyway.

My fist clenched. I almost didn't care. It sort of made me feel like a jerk, but I really almost didn't care. I was tired of this. I wanted an answer. I wanted to be with her. And I didn't want to keep making a fool of myself if that wasn't going to happen.

But I also didn't want to push her and end up driving her away by default.

I scowled, my head starting to ache, and not just from the infuriating situation currently turning my brain into a pretzel. I hadn't lied. Things didn't hurt the same when my greliaran side took over. But that didn't mean they didn't hurt at *all*, and after spending the better part of the morning fighting my cousins, a few of the punches were really beginning to make me sore.

The country roads turned finally to a highway and Baylie headed south. It wouldn't be more than a few hours till we reached this Joseph guy's house; in the scope of the entire continent, he lived ridiculously close to my cousins, all things considered. At first, I'd worried that fact might mean he was connected to them in some way, except that Dad would have told us if Richard knew the guy who'd actually *made* greliarans, and who was somehow still alive after all these centuries. I couldn't imagine that my uncle or cousins wouldn't have let *that* slip.

It was too incredible for words, and not in a good way.

I shifted uncomfortably on the seat. I knew what we were. What we'd been created to do. It was just a thing, something we had to deal with – or not – and it wasn't important except where it could get us into trouble.

But to meet the guy who'd actually *made* us this way…

Who'd wanted dehaians dead so much that he and his friends created an entire *species* just to wipe them out…

I swallowed. I wished there was another option besides going to see him, for so many reasons.

Following the directions Dave had relayed to her on our drive cross-country, Ellie helped Baylie navigate down the highways and then eventually back onto more country roads. The smell of salt carried through the air, growing stronger while we wound toward the ocean again. According to Dave, Joseph lived right on the coast – a fact I found disturbing. I knew why my cousins lived there. It didn't bode well that Joseph did too.

We continued down the back roads, with trees closing in around us and gravel growling beneath the tires so similarly to the last place on the coast we'd left behind. No other side paths led off through the trees this time, however, leaving us trapped on the only trail through the forest. I eyed the woods cautiously, watching for an ambush and seeing nothing but greenery and fallen logs.

And sculptures.

I paused, my gaze catching on the short pillars dotting either side of the road, just behind the first layer of trees and undergrowth. Like survey markers, they were spaced every few hundred feet. Dotted with moisture and moss, the concrete posts looked as though they'd stood in the woods for years, to the point where I couldn't make out much of the weathered carvings on their sides.

My eyes tracked across them as we drove past. They could be nothing.

I somehow doubted that.

The car drove on, tracing the winding gravel road.

In the seat next to me, Chloe twitched. I glanced over. She hesitated, spotting the questioning look on my face.

"Air feels weird," she said quietly.

My brow drew down. I looked at the road ahead.

A moment passed. My caution turned to alarm.

She was right. Something was… not *wrong*, exactly. Weird was the best term. Like a warm, prickling sensation wherever the air touched me. As the seconds passed, it seemed to grow, spreading through my body and filling my mind with a heady, dizzying rush.

It made me feel so alive.

Quivers shook my muscles, and I tensed. The greliaran side of me felt stronger in this too, as though the very air fed it energy. It wanted to take over, to draw in everything of this it could. My heart started to pound harder while heat spread through my skin. I drew a slow breath, fighting to keep control.

Chloe shifted on the seat. I couldn't stop my gaze from snapping toward the motion. Below her jean shorts, she rubbed absently at her thigh, and I could see swirls of iridescence brushing her skin.

"Hey, you guys doing alright?" Baylie called, glancing at the rearview mirror.

"How much longer?" I asked, barely managing to keep the growl from my voice.

Baylie tossed a quick look to Ellie.

"I-I think we're almost there," the girl answered, sounding distracted.

"What's wrong?" Chloe asked her.

"Just a bit carsick," Ellie replied in the same tone.

Chloe glanced toward me. I turned away before she could meet my gaze.

Colors were getting sharper. This wasn't good.

I closed my eyes. I wouldn't lose control in this… this *whatever* it was. And if that bastard had put something here to make us all change…

Shivers coursed through me. I pushed the anger away. It was just making things worse.

Carefully, I took another breath.

My heartbeat slowed. The heat below my skin cooled and my greliaran impulses settled back inside.

I opened my eyes.

The dull world met my gaze. The air still felt just as odd, but it wasn't as overwhelming as before, almost like I'd adjusted to it somehow. Swallowing hard, I glanced to Chloe.

She'd closed her eyes too. I could see her trembling.

"Chloe?"

She made a tight noise, shaking her head. Her fingers clutched her legs while furrows lined her brow.

In the front seat, Ellie twisted to look back at us. "Is she–"

"I'm fine," Chloe snapped through gritted teeth.

I hesitated. That didn't exactly look true.

A shudder ran through her and scales began to form on her legs. She tensed, something almost like rage flashing over her face.

The scales became skin again. A heartbeat passed, and then the iridescence disappeared as well.

Unsteadily, Chloe drew a breath. She opened her eyes, blinking a few times before turning her gaze to mine. Radiant green flecked her irises like glints from an emerald, but after a moment, the glow faded.

"What the *hell?*" she whispered.

I shook my head, watching her. Bloodlessly pale, she was still shaking and her breathing was ragged.

Before I could stop myself, I reached over again, taking her hand.

She didn't move away this time. Her fingers laced through mine, and her grip trembled while she squeezed my hand tightly.

"You guys sure you're okay?" Baylie asked.

"Yeah," I said, still keeping an eye to Chloe. She nodded, her gaze back on her legs as though she was holding them in human form by sheer force of will.

"Weird, but alright," Ellie replied.

"Does it hurt being this close to the water?" Chloe asked, glancing up sharply.

Ellie shook her head. "No, no it's not like that. Just… shaky." She swallowed hard. "I'm fine."

A heartbeat passed, but no one said anything else. Taking a deep breath, I looked to the road ahead, grateful for being able to touch Chloe again, even if for *nothing* else that had just happened. The tree cover looked like it was thinning, and I caught glimpses of gray sky through the trunks. Beyond the growl of the tires on the gravel, the white-noise rush of waves carried through the salt-heavy air.

And meanwhile, the short pillars still dotted the roadside.

I eyed them warily. I couldn't be certain – the moss was too thick – but the symbols on the sides looked different.

The car came around a turn and the tree cover fell away, leaving us on a barren expanse several hundred yards from a cliff. Gravel stretched around us without a weed or shred of grass to be seen, and at the edge of it, a two-story house stood so close to the cliff's edge, it seemed a miracle the building hadn't fallen into the sea. Stonework formed the house's foundation, which rose nearly half a story high, and then a wide porch marked the line where white siding began. The porch wrapped around the entire building while a black roof formed the house's top.

Baylie pulled the car to a stop. Nothing moved but the ocean and the wind in the trees. On the side of the house, tall windows looked back at us, reflecting the forest and revealing nothing of what lay inside. There wasn't a car in the driveway—or even a driveway to speak of, for that matter – and when the noise from the engine died, no sound but the rushing of the waves took its place.

"So, um," Baylie tried while she tugged the keys from the ignition. "I don't suppose we should wait for Robin and Dave?"

Chloe drew a slow breath and I saw her glance toward the ocean, tension on her face. "They could be hours. Let's just knock on the door. See if he's willing to help."

Her gaze flicked to the water again. I resisted the urge to ask if she felt anything strange coming from it.

But I could read between the lines of what she said. If Joseph wouldn't help, getting out of here fast would be the best plan. There was no telling when this Beast thing might pick up on her.

Reluctantly, I released her hand and then pushed open the door. Shutting it behind me, I scanned the area warily and then headed for the steps, staying close to Chloe. I kept an eye to her while I went, in case her legs started to change again, and on the other side of her I could see Baylie doing the same thing.

"What is it?" Baylie whispered. "Something weird out there?"

"No," Chloe answered just as softly.

"Then what?" Baylie pressed.

"Zeke. He should be here already."

"Maybe he's inside?"

Chloe didn't respond.

I kept walking. Dark wood creaked under my shoes as I climbed to the porch, and equally dark wood greeted us at the door. With a glance to the windows nearby, I lifted a hand and knocked.

The door opened before I finished, revealing the oddest person I'd ever seen.

He looked like a turtle, and not just because of the lopsided hump that seemed to form the majority of his back. His face was scaly, his skin was a pale shade of green, and his nose seemed more a pointed lump than anything else. His lips were a dark and vaguely bony line on his face, and he barely had a chin to speak of. Though his left eye was brown and mostly normal, his right was black as a ball of onyx. On his head, his gray hair stood out like the fronds of some undersea plant. He wore a shapeless, maroon robe that shared more in common with an old woman's polyester muumuu than anything, and at least twenty bits of jewelry dangled from him, ranging from necklaces of crystals to bracelets of various metals.

I tried to keep from staring. He was like a disconcerting mash-up of stereotypical wizardry and cartoon animals.

"Well?" he demanded. "What are you waiting for? Get inside already."

Scuttling back from the door, he motioned impatiently for us to come in.

I cast a quick look to the girls. "Are you Joseph?" I asked him.

"No, I'm some other guy living right where Dave told you

to find me," he retorted. "Geez, so much for hoping that a few centuries would give you greliarans some brains."

I tensed. "What do you–"

The man made an irritated noise. With a gnarled finger, he pointed at all of us in rapid succession. "Greliaran. Landwalker. Human. Dehaian – sort of. You think I'd miss something like you all coming toward my house? You're the damned United Nations of Species, for pity's sake. Half the reason I let you through was to see how a carload of people like you all was even possible. I assume you're doing it?"

He directed the last to Chloe.

She hesitated and then gave a small shrug. "I helped her," she replied, nodding toward Ellie.

He made a harrumphing sound and looked Ellie up and down for a heartbeat before doing the same to me. "Well, come in, then."

Cautiously, I walked inside. Wood paneling lined the walls, floor and ceiling alike, making the hallway feel like a tunnel, and above the staircase to my right, nothing of the second story was visible. On my left, a large room extended farther back into the house, its floor slightly sunken from the hallway's level. Assorted tables filled the space at random angles, while sprawled across and between them was such an arrangement of tubes, pipettes and beakers, it looked like a chemist's lab gone berserk. Bunsen burners dotted the tabletops and liquids in countless shades bubbled in the containers above them. Sheets of translucent glass hung from chains on the walls, and in them, the reflected flames seemed to move in disconcerting ways. Over the tables, vent fans were lodged in the ceiling, their blades spinning idly behind metal screens.

Joseph shut the door and I looked back. For a heartbeat, he regarded the wood, and then pounded a fist to a spot near the top corner. Making a satisfied noise, he turned to the hall.

"This way," he said shortly, pushing past us. Waddling down the step to the large room, he didn't look back but just continued into the chemical chaos.

I stared after him, not sure what to feel. Some part of me wanted to laugh, but it wasn't really funny. This was him. The guy who'd made greliarans.

The turtle who'd made greliarans.

I shook my head in disbelief and then glanced to the girls. Her gaze on the beakers and tubes, Chloe looked like she was reconsidering the plan.

Reaching out, I put a hand to her arm.

She drew a breath as if she hadn't taken one since we'd walked in the door. "I'm fine," she said tightly, not looking at me.

I hesitated, unconvinced, but she just started after Joseph. With a glance to Baylie, I followed, staying close to Chloe's side. At the rear of the room, Joseph stood by a heavily locked wooden door, eyeing us with exasperation. When we came closer, he turned back, taking a ring of keys from inside his robes. In rapid succession, he inserted the keys into the row of metal locks on the dark wood, and then grabbed the latch and pushed the door wide.

My brow rose. I'd thought the last room was strange.

The floor was stone, and the walls were too. An enormous machine sat in the middle of the room, sunken into a circular space in the floor like a shallow and oversized well. Tarnished brass made up the majority of the machine's body, the heart of which was cylindrical like a massive canister. Smaller brass canisters clung to its side like growths, connected to each other and the main container by a rat's nest of pipes. Additional pipes, larger and thicker than the rest, ran up from the various, bolted-down lids through the ceiling or stretched from the machine's base and into the walls like roots on some metal tree. Gauges protruded from everywhere, each one marked with strange symbols and monitoring nothing I could determine. A hissing sound I somehow hadn't heard at all from the other room filtered from the machine, mixed with popping noises like the gaskets were barely holding under pressure.

"This way, this way," Joseph prompted again.

He headed past the machine to a desk in the back of the room. A collection of a half dozen chairs butted up against each other in a corner nearby, like every seat in the house had congregated there for safety in numbers, and most of them held stacks of books.

"Don't get many visitors," Joseph muttered by way of explanation while he relocated the books to the floor.

We scooted the chairs farther from the corner, while Joseph leaned on the edge of his desk.

Chloe hesitated, her hands clutching the top of a wooden chair. "So no one else came by today before us? Like, maybe some dehaians?"

"What I just said, wasn't it? I don't do social."

Swallowing hard, she nodded at the obvious statement and then sat down.

His normal eye twitching back and forth, Joseph regarded us. "Damned United Nations," he muttered. "You let that crazy side of you out, I'll show you what we did to wild greliarans in my day."

He aimed the last at me.

I paused, not certain how to respond. "I won't," I managed.

Baylie glanced between us. "Yeah, okay… Well, um, Dave said you could help us. Her."

"Oh, he did, did he?" Joseph replied. "Landwalkers. Think everything is just so easy. No clue what magic involves."

Ellie shifted uncomfortably.

"Don't get all offended, girl," he continued. "You'll be better at your tricks than any of them, once you grow up a bit and get a handle on what's inside you. But that doesn't mean the others aren't idiots."

Ellie's brow drew down.

Joseph snorted.

"So can you help?" I hazarded when he didn't say anything more.

"Well, of course I can. Take a bit though. I have to get things ready."

"I thought you knew we were coming," Chloe said.

"*Yes*," he acknowledged pedantically, "but that doesn't mean that I can just flip a switch and presto, make you like her or the ones out there." He jerked his head at Ellie and then in the direction of the ocean. "This is complicated magic we're talking about. Even the dehaians took years to get it right – and lost more than a few of their kind in the process. Now, that's not going to happen here, but only if I adjust the procedure to your body chemistry just right."

Chloe appeared paler than normal. "How long?"

"About ten minutes."

The words were met with incredulous expressions.

"What?"

"That's *basically* flipping a switch," Baylie allowed.

"No, flipping a switch is instantaneous. Ten minutes isn't. Ten minutes is me studying magic for centuries and being damn good at what I do."

Chloe cleared her throat. "So is there any way to control which… which side I'll be?"

Joseph shrugged. "Not that I know of. Whole families got split up when the old dehaians did it, so I heard. Why, you have a favorite or something?"

Chloe didn't respond. I glanced over. She looked sick.

"Why should we trust you?" I asked. "You created greliarans to kill people like her. Either way she goes, she's still your–"

"I know what she is," Joseph interrupted, "same as I know what you are. I've been keeping her kind safe from yours for years."

I stared at him.

"You think it's an *accident* the greliarans haven't hardly found a dehaian in decades? I've been doing my *damnedest* to keep dehaians from wandering near greliaran houses. I even had a deal worked out with the landwalkers about it. Every time they relocated greliarans to the coast, they were supposed to let me know so I could keep tabs on those greliarans and confuse their senses about any dehaians nearby. Worked great, too, till the landwalkers screwed up and forgot to tell me about one family. A guy and his teenage daughter. Without me stopping them, those two got their hands on a dehaian practically overnight. Tried to filet the bastard, he defended himself by making the kid fall for him, and next thing you know, the daddy's offed the dehaian and the girl's killed herself because she can't live without her new boyfriend. And all because the damn landwalkers forgot to make a phone call."

Chloe tensed. I glanced to her.

"Earl," she said. "The guy who attacked us at Baylie's place."

"You've met him?" Joseph asked.

Chloe hesitated. "We stumbled on his house a few weeks ago."

Joseph scoffed. "You're a right mess, you know that? Can't track you, and you screw up the magical signature of everything you come near. I would've kept you from going near there, but I can't find up from down in the soup you've made. You sent my monitoring systems all to hell a couple months back. There were power surges that vanished as fast as they came, ghost readings first here, then there. All sorts of chaos, and it hasn't much stopped. And the Beast obviously isn't dead yet, because the bastard picked up on it too. If you're as good with this stuff as I am – and as that damn creature is – there's no way you don't notice that."

I studied him distrustfully. Rants and cursing aside, the turtle wizard obviously liked to hear himself talk. Whether or not he 'did social', he'd clearly been on his own for a long time and now, with visitors, he'd become a geyser of one-sided conversation.

But he hadn't answered the question. And given the reasons that we, the species he'd made, liked to get our hands on dehaians, that made me nervous.

"But why are you protecting them?" I asked. "Why should we trust you?"

"Because I need every one of her kind I can get."

I tensed. "What does that mean?"

His expression turned withering. "Just that her lot screwed up the world when they did their little 'splitting themselves' trick. Magic is complicated. Like everything else, it's part of an ecosystem, and when you take out a component of that, you break things. The ocean generates magic. Why do you think humans are so drawn to it? Why dehaians need it? Hell, even you need it to some degree." He jerked his chin at me. "And the dehaians – the old ones – they helped that process of magic generation by going back and forth between land and sea. They created an exchange of energy – carried the magic with them like some damn bug with pollen on its body – and thus they kept things from stagnating and dying. Not that they cared, the selfish pricks. They'd already damn near destroyed everything with that 'Beast' of theirs. But when they split themselves apart like that, they altered the whole thing."

He scowled. "And that screwed my kind over too. I made it through their first apocalypse by being off-island with some friends at the time. Saw it from a distance though. Bastards." He shook his head. "And I did everything possible to avoid their Beast in the years after that. But once the dehaians split…" He made an angry noise. "To do what I do, I need access to magic. It's kind of a big part of being a wizard. And it takes a lot, keeping yourself going after centuries. I've used what we learned from creating greliarans to help that–" he gestured to his face, "–though of course, my targets were long-lived creatures and the like, rather than the rabid concoction that went into you lot. But I still need magic to survive. My machines distill out what they can from the ocean water, and I can modify it to be like the old world magic to some extent in my laboratory, but the amount of energy I get from all that is pathetic compared to what it used to be. The dehaians don't bring out much from the water, can't travel far enough inland to carry energy from those places back with them, and regardless it's not the same. The whole magical ecosystem isn't the same – like they took saltwater and turned it into fresh. But the dehaians *do* still keep things going in *some* form, and without them, the ocean's magic would just die out entirely. So you see, I can't let the greliarans kill them off. Like I said, I need every one of them I can get."

I watched him, not sure I was buying that. "But you made us to kill them. If this magical exchange is so important, why do that?"

"That was different," Joseph replied like I was an idiot for asking. "We were defending ourselves. I mean, what would *you* do if you found yourself suddenly at war with a bunch of incredibly strong, incredibly fast, spiky-armed nightmares who could make you adore them with a touch? I mean, one minute you're fighting side-by-side with your buddy, and the next he's trying to kill you because you're attacking the new love of his life. We *had* to counter that. Our leaders *ordered* us to counter that. So yeah, we took dehaian prisoners and human volunteers and every magical trace element we could gather from animals and nature on the islands… and we created you. Gave you strength and speed to fight them, skin to handle their spikes, and hearing and a sense of each other's location so that – if those bastards dragged one of you underwater – it'd give the others a hope of saving him and killing the dehaian responsible. We made you with all that, plus a craving to absorb the magical energy dehaians give off when they die that was *so* strong, it'd stand a chance of overriding any love magic they tried. Didn't matter that it left you all as psychotic as serial killers, or that you couldn't understand anything but brute force to keep you in line. It was necessary. Back then, it was necessary. Now, you're just a throwback to a bygone era that refuses to die off."

I stared at him, uncertain whether to be more angry or shocked.

"Shut up," Baylie ordered.

Joseph glanced to her. "What? Is he your boyfriend?"

"Stepbrother, you jerk. And if you keep talking about him like that, I'll–"

"Yeah, well, your stepbrother shouldn't even be able to stay in the same room as her. Not without twitching like an addict in desperate need of a hit. I know what he is. I made his kind, and he's got just as much of that in him as the rest do. He should be going crazy, and if he's not, that doesn't mean he won't eventually."

I tensed.

"She said shut up," Chloe snapped.

Joseph regarded me for another moment and then his gaze flicked to the girls, taking in the anger on their faces. "Damned United Nations," he muttered again. He gave them an exasperated look. "Listen, I'm not telling you anything he doesn't already know is true."

"It's not true about me," I said, carefully keeping my voice calm.

He hesitated and then harrumphed again. Pushing away from the desk, he straightened. "Whatever you say. I have work to do."

I drew a breath.

He circled the desk and then tugged open a drawer. From

inside, he pulled out the white box of a first aid kit, though the thing was held closed with string and appeared to be nearly bursting at the seams. With quick motions, he untied the string and then took a plastic-sealed syringe from inside.

"Just a bit of blood to begin the process," he said while he examined the syringe.

He waddled back around the desk to Chloe's side. She shifted like she wanted to pull away.

"Don't move," he cautioned.

She nodded, the motion tight and jerky.

Joseph ignored it. Unwrapping the needle, he checked over it one more time and then stuck it into her arm.

Blood began to fill the syringe.

Chloe turned her face away, closing her eyes.

Seconds passed. He removed the needle and pressed a wad of gauze to the inside of her arm.

"There. Hold that."

She did as ordered.

Joseph set the syringe down and then retrieved a strip of medical tape. Quickly, he stuck it across the gauze and then turned, grabbing a pair of scissors from the box. Chloe flinched back in surprise when he snipped off a lock of her hair.

"Alright," he said. "That should get me started."

He shoved both the needle and the hair into the first aid kit. Hefting the box beneath one arm, and losing a few random bandages from its sides in the process, he headed for the door.

Ellie twisted in the seat. "Wait. Is this safe, though? Us

being here while you work on that, I mean. We're so close to the water, and if the Beast picks up on her…"

Joseph tossed her a derisive look. "First off, that thing was targeted at my kind, and I've been here for decades. We're fine. Second, I'm guessing your friend is muffling the magical energy coming from her just about as tightly as she can, am I right?"

He eyed Chloe, waiting.

She gave a small shrug. "I guess."

"Yeah, well, with you hiding like that, you're fine here. You could even go in the ocean and, if you got lucky and the Beast was far enough away, you wouldn't attract it even if it was back at full strength. Not right away, in any case. And keeping folks like her," he nodded to Ellie, "or dehaians around makes you safer still. Disrupts the signal you're sending off and makes you harder to track."

"What does that mean?" she asked.

His withering expression returned. "Okay, it's like this," he sighed. "You're energy. I'm energy. Every damn thing in the world is energy. And that energy has a variety of frequencies. Signatures. Things that make you different than, say, a cauliflower. The Beast is tuned only to those frequencies that are unique to old dehaians and to wizards like me. Just those. It ignores greliarans, because apparently, the dehaians aimed it at us first. Probably thought to get the creators of the weapons before we could make more. But then they lost control of the damn thing and it turned on them too."

He scoffed. "Bastards. But regardless, the Beast is drawn to those specific signatures – and you're close enough to that old signature to wake the thing up. But the current dehaians and landwalkers, the Beast ignores them. They're basically invisible to it. They're still putting off energy, though, and just like two songs playing in the same room make it harder to listen to one, their signal disrupts yours. More of them around you, the better off you are – which probably is *also* why I've had such trouble getting a lock on you, if you've been around them and the dehaians all this time." He glared at Chloe briefly before falling back into his surly, lecturing mode. "But meanwhile, muffled up and trying to hide as you are, you're sending out the energy of, say, a candle. When you stop hiding, you're the damn sun. If the Beast is close, it'll spot you either way. But if it's not… well, it's harder to spot a candle at a distance than a star, right?"

Chloe's brow furrowed at all the metaphors. "Um, alright, but how do I even know if it's close?"

He chuckled. "Well, once it's strong enough, you'd know mostly because you'd be dying. But until then… you'd want to watch for changes around you. Weird feelings in the air and water, like you're getting weaker and you don't know why. That means it's got your scent and you better run – or swim – for your life."

Chloe swallowed hard.

"But it's not an issue," Joseph continued. "I'm going to change up your magic same as your ancestors did theirs. And until then, I've got enough shielding around my property that you could stop muffling yourself up with the Beast right outside and it still wouldn't pick up on you. What do you think you all passed out there?" He snorted derisively. "You probably didn't even see the markers in the forest. The concrete–"

"The little pillar things, yeah," I interrupted. "We saw them."

"Huh. Well, those form protective barriers. Layers of them. Every trace of magical leakage from my machines is trapped, so there's nothing for the Beast to pick up on."

"That's what we drove through?" Ellie asked. "The weird feeling in the air?"

"Basically the magical equivalent of instantly going up a few thousand feet in elevation – except it probably won't kill you and you adjust to it faster. But that shielding will hold, even if I let you drive through it. Magic leakage might make it past a few barriers, but it can't get by *every* one. And the house is even more secure, meaning that as long as you're in it," he looked pointedly to Chloe, "the Beast won't have a chance in hell of knowing you're here."

Ellie fidgeted on the chair. I glanced to her. She had that look on her face again – the nervous one, like she wanted to say something but wasn't sure it'd be okay.

Chloe seemed to see the expression as well. "What is it?"

Ellie looked her way and then hesitated, catching sight of me. She dropped her gaze quickly, almost as if she was uncomfortable meeting my eyes.

I tried not to scowl, mentally thanking the turtle for making Ellie frightened of me on top of everything else.

"It's just, you said Chloe messes your stuff up," Ellie explained to Joseph. "Couldn't she do that to your barriers?"

Joseph paused, and then harrumphed again. "It'll be fine. I know what I'm doing."

He waddled back toward the other room, leaving us sitting beside the desk.

"Why doesn't that reassure me?" Baylie muttered under her breath.

I looked over to her. Baylie's lip twitched when she realized I'd heard, though the smile died quickly.

"We'll keep an eye out," I told her. "If something starts to seem off or you feel anything strange," I glanced to Chloe, "we'll leave."

Chloe hesitated, her gaze on the desk in front of her, though it didn't seem like she was seeing it. "Yeah," she agreed distantly.

My brow drew down.

She seemed to feel my curiosity. A weird, pained expression flickered across her face. Without looking my way, she shoved up from the chair and hurried after Joseph.

I watched her leave and then turned to Baylie, confused.

"I'll go talk to her," Baylie said.

She followed Chloe from the room.

I took a deep breath. Chloe couldn't be scared of me too. She knew what I was, but whatever that turtle said, she had to know I'd never hurt her.

At least, I hoped she did.

"So, um… he's kind of a jerk, yeah?" Ellie asked, more than the regular share of nervousness in her tone.

I glanced to her. She eyed me askance, like she felt awkward about looking at me.

"Yeah," I replied flatly.

I gave her a tight smile and then pushed out of the chair, heading for the door. I needed air. Space. Something.

And I wished we'd never come to this place.

20

WYATT

Owen pulled the SUV to a stop.

The landwalkers were ahead of us, standing beside a brown sedan with their attention on a gravel track leading farther into the woods.

"You think they found them already?" Clay asked.

"It's another five miles to where that guy said she'd be," Owen pointed out.

I ignored them both, watching the landwalkers. Only one car was parked ahead, with the other two sedans nowhere to be seen. All the guys who'd been on the road near our house were gone too, with only that scrawny lab assistant and the round, old cop remaining. They weren't doing well, either. The cop clung to the sedan like it was the rock holding him stable against the spinning world, while the toothpick guy just looked like he was about to shake apart. Neither of them reacted to our SUV pulling up near them, though perhaps they were in too much pain to care anymore.

And then there was Harman.

His hands shook when he pointed to the forest, and I could see the sweat dripping down his face like he was under intense stress or strain.

Not that he seemed to notice. Pacing back and forth in front of the turnoff, he appeared to be speaking. Every few moments, he'd start down the road, only to suddenly retreat.

I pushed open the passenger door, still studying him.

He *was* talking, though his voice was so low that it couldn't be meant for the others to hear. In rambling mutters, he was going on about how this had to work, about the other men collapsing, and about medicines holding out because he had a mission. Research. Lives to save. When we came closer, he turned. My brow rose at the look on his face.

I'd seen crazy. Much time around the more pathetic of the older greliarans, and you sort of became used to the way those aging weaklings cracked.

But I'd never seen anything like this.

His eyes were practically sparkling. His mouth twitched in and out of a spasmodic smile like the muscles couldn't agree on which ones needed to work for the expression to hold. He didn't really seem to see us, and his gaze kept returning to the forest like it was pulled there by a string.

"What–" the large cop sputtered when he finally spotted us.

He grabbed for his gun.

"No," Harman protested, hurrying back from the side road. "No, no it's fine."

"How is it *fine?*" the cop demanded. "These things, they… they're not landwalkers. They're not even *human*. They're–what the hell *are* they?"

Harman appeared to barely hear the question. His gaze stuttered toward the other road.

"G-greliarans," the scrawny assistant guy supplied, eyeing us like he wanted to back away. "They're, um… they were created to kill dehaians and–"

"*What?*" the cop snapped. "Harman, Chloe Kowalski is half–"

"It's fine," the doctor interrupted, his gaze snapping to us again. "It's just fine."

Harman shuffled toward us quickly. "She's down the road," he said to me. "You have to help us reach her. We can't seem to get to her. Every time we drive there, we end up back here. The road. It bends. It…" He looked up at me, that crazy light in his eyes growing stronger. "You have to save Chloe, Richard. And Eleanor too."

My brow climbed again. Wait… *Richard?* Seriously?

"I don't want these things involved, Doctor Brooks," the cop insisted. "This madness has gone far enough. This is a matter for landwalkers, so send those creatures back where they came from and let us rescue the girls ourselves."

I barely held back a growl. There was no way in hell that was happening. I'd break his fat neck if he tried to stop me from killing that bitch.

"No," Harman argued, "they have to help, Barry. These are

the *good* ones. The dehaian boy, that other greliaran boy, *they're* the ones who are against us. They want to push Chloe into giving up every trace of humanity she has left. They've filled her head with… with stories. Lies. She doesn't understand the danger of all this because of them. But these…" He attempted to look at us, but his crazy gaze didn't seem able to make the trip before it returned to the side road. "Richard and his sons will help us. They can stop those boys and bring Chloe to safety."

Appearing more unsettled by the second, the assistant glanced from Harman to us as if he couldn't decide whether to tell the old man that he had our identities wrong.

The cop only grimaced, however. "Fine," he agreed, his tone strained. "But for her safety, she's coming back in our vehicle. All the girls are."

"Of course," Harman said.

I eyed them. Again, that wouldn't happen. But arguing here wouldn't fix it.

Making it clear how wrong they were once I had the fish girl in my grasp, on the other hand…

I restrained a smirk.

"I need more medicine," the cop muttered. He headed around to the other side of the sedan.

"D-Doctor Brooks?" the scrawny assistant tried. "About the treatments, though… what your granddaughter said–"

"Eleanor is *confused*, Aaron," Harman stated as if he couldn't believe the other guy didn't see it. "My treatments save lives.

They *always* save lives, and with Chloe's help, they'll save even more. It's vital we keep her from losing herself by becoming any more like those soulless creatures than she already has. Our research *depends* upon it."

Aaron's brow furrowed. Seeming discomfited, he dropped his gaze away.

"Now, Richard," Harman continued to me. "Can you see about this road? We simply *must* reach her soon."

I regarded him flatly, but he'd already returned to watching the forest and talking to himself.

Psycho.

Suppressing a scoff, I steered clear of him and walked toward the gravel track.

My feet stopped almost immediately. There was something wrong with the air. It seemed to vibrate, as if an enormous speaker waited ahead of me, playing on full blast. But I couldn't hear a thing. Only the regular sounds of the forest surrounded me, interrupted sporadically by Harman's muttering. The farther I continued down the side road, though, the worse it became — like the world was trying to bend around me.

I retreated several steps. The warped feeling faded a bit.

Thoughtfully, I studied the road. Whatever it was, magic had to be involved. Humans couldn't do this. Humans wouldn't even know where to begin.

"What is it?" Owen asked.

I didn't respond. If it was magic, then maybe we could take it. Kill whatever was causing it and absorb it into ourselves.

This much power… it'd probably feel *amazing*.

I looked to Owen. "It–"

The vibration around me shifted. I turned back to the forest.

Nothing had changed.

Except I could tell that wasn't right. Something had shifted. Birds still chirped and creatures still moved through the undergrowth… but the vibrations around me didn't feel quite the same.

"Get the car," I ordered.

Clay made a confused noise. "But what about–"

"I said get the car."

I scanned the forest while Clay crunched away on the gravel, heading for the SUV. I wasn't sure what'd just happened, but it didn't really matter. The girl was on the other side of this, and something felt like it'd changed.

That was enough for me. Time to find that bitch and finally give me a fish to kill.

21

CHLOE

I rushed out of the room and almost ran straight into Joseph.

"Careful!" he snapped, retreating a step while I came to a sharp stop.

"Sorry." I glanced around. "Do you have a restroom I could use?"

He eyed me balefully and then jerked his head toward the entry. "Down the hall, first door on the right."

"Thanks."

I fled the room. Baylie would be coming after me. Or Noah, God forbid. I didn't want to talk to either of them. I didn't even know what to say.

The bathroom door was nearly indistinguishable from the dark wood siding on the hallway walls. If not for the doorknob, I would've missed it entirely. Fumbling at the handle, I pushed the door open and then hurried inside, shutting it behind me.

Closing my eyes, I leaned back, resting my head on the wood.

I was being ridiculous. I'd known that there was a chance I

wouldn't be able to choose what I became. I'd come here anyway, because Joseph was my only shot at stopping all this.

But I didn't want to end up a landwalker. I didn't want this to be the last time I saw the ocean.

Or Zeke and Noah.

A breath left me, the sound ragged. Zeke couldn't leave the ocean. I knew that, obviously. And as for Noah… I'd heard Joseph. Greliarans needed the sea too. Not like dehaians, not to the point where they couldn't *ever* travel inland, but they did. Noah had said something like that once, back when he was driving me to the ocean with the Sylphaen's drugs in my blood. He'd said it felt better to be near the sea.

Thrusting away from the door, I crossed to the sink. I turned on the tap and watched the water rush into the drain for a moment before splashing it onto my face.

I was being stupid. Nothing had happened yet. There was every possibility I could become dehaian. Sure, it was a gamble, but it was a fifty-fifty chance. Lots of people didn't get those odds in life.

My gaze lifted to the mirror. And if I didn't become dehaian like Zeke, I'd never see him or the ocean again, and the chance for any kind of relationship between me and Noah was as good as gone. I'd have to stay with my parents, or somewhere inland, and figure out how to live when everything remotely close to the ocean was pretty much off-limits to me.

I snagged a hand towel and scrubbed it over my face, fighting the tears burning in my eyes. This was stupid too. I could still date Noah. If he wanted to be with me, anyway. But hey, long-distance relationships… well, sometimes they worked, though probably not *forever*. And as for Zeke… okay, so I'd never get to say goodbye. So the thought of that made me want to throw up. So I didn't even know where he *was* and I couldn't stop worrying about what that could *mean*, since he *really* should have been here by now, and–

A knock on the bathroom door made me jump, and spikes rushed from my arms to topple a bottle on the edge of the sink. The plastic thing clattered to the ground.

"Chloe?" Baylie called.

I snatched the bottle from the floor and returned it to the counter before turning off the faucet. Drawing a breath, I crossed the small space, swiping tears away while I went.

She eyed me warily when I opened the door. "You okay?"

I nodded.

Her mouth thinned. Giving the hall a quick glance, she slipped into the bathroom with me.

"What is it?" she asked after she shut the door.

I shook my head.

"Chloe."

"It's dumb."

"Okay. Tell me anyway."

I looked down. "It's just… the landwalker thing."

"Maybe becoming one of them, you mean?"

I nodded.

She paused, taking a slow breath. "You'll be dehaian," she

said with certainty. "It'll be fine."

I gave her a skeptical look.

"Oh, come on. If you want it that badly, I'm sure you will."

"I lived like a landwalker for my whole life, though. Up till these past few weeks, anyway. What if that… I don't know… *did* something? Made that side stronger?"

"What if it didn't?"

I grimaced.

"You'll be dehaian. And if you're not, well…" She cleared her throat. "Hey, we could go to college in Colorado, right? That was the backup plan if California didn't work out. We'll get an apartment like we always talked about and take classes together and throw crazy parties." She smiled, a tinge of hope in her eyes. "That wouldn't be so bad."

I hesitated. "Do you *want* me to be a landwalker?"

"What? No, of course not! You want to be dehaian. I get that."

"Baylie."

"What?"

My brow twitched up.

"I don't!"

I waited.

"I want you to be happy," she insisted. "And it'd suck to get sick like them."

"Dehaians get sick too. I… I couldn't come more than maybe a hundred miles inland if I was one of them. Like they are now, I mean. And I'd have to go back underwater every few weeks or so, at least."

"Yeah, no, I-I know that," she said with an awkward shrug.

There was something weird in her tone. I leaned back on the counter, watching her. "Baylie?"

Her brow furrowed. She reached over to fidget with the frayed edge of a bath towel. "You know how, when we were kids, we talked about how we'd have houses next door to each other when we grew up?"

"I remember we planned secret tunnels leading from one house to the other."

Her lip twitched. "Yeah, that too." The smile died. "It's just, if you're like you are now, that can't happen. None of the things we talked about can. And if you're dehaian… it's the same. But if you're a landwalker, I know you'd be miserable."

"I'd deal," I managed.

She gave me a pained look. "I don't want you to be unhappy. I just…" She dropped her gaze to the tile floor. "I kind of don't want to lose all that either."

I swallowed. "Neither do I."

She nodded, her attention still on the tiles.

Shifting uncomfortably against the counter, I drew a breath. "We could still get an apartment if I'm like the other dehaians, though. And take classes together and all that. I'd just, you know, have to slip off to the beach every so often. We could even have houses near each other like we wanted."

Baylie smiled, sadness in the expression. "You're not going to need a house, Chloe. Or some college degree. Not if you're like them."

I looked away.

The silence stretched.

"What about Noah?" Baylie asked quietly.

I tried to keep from grimacing.

"What's up with that, Chloe? Noah… he *really* likes you. And I thought you liked him too. But now you have this Zeke guy around, and–"

"It's not like that," I protested. "I didn't plan this. I'm not trying to hurt Noah. Or Zeke. I–"

"What *happened*?"

I struggled for words. "It got complicated."

She waited, her brow twitching up.

I didn't know what to say. "I just–"

A shiver ran through me, like a current of icy air had suddenly brushed my skin.

Baylie saw my expression change. "What?"

I didn't respond, my gaze turning toward the wall and the ocean beyond while my heart started to pound. I knew this feeling. It'd been a lifetime ago, near Santa Lucina, but I'd felt this before.

It couldn't be. Joseph said we were safe here.

Ellie said I might screw up his defenses.

"Chloe?"

I pushed past Baylie and tugged open the door. I ran down the hall, catching myself on the entry to Joseph's laboratory.

He looked up in alarm.

"Did you feel that?" I asked.

He regarded me with annoyance. "Feel wha…" Color drained from his green skin while his mismatched eyes went wide.

"Where are Noah and Ellie?" I demanded.

Ellie walked from the other room. "What's wrong?"

Joseph ignored me. "How? I checked everything. It–"

He rushed toward the glass panes on his wall.

Ellie glanced between us. "I think Noah went outside."

I yanked open the front door and raced onto the porch.

Noah came running around the side of the house. "Chloe!"

I hurried down the steps. "You felt that?"

His brow furrowed. "What? No. But we've got to go." He jerked his head toward the ocean and then looked to Baylie. "Keys?"

She tugged them from her pocket and tossed them to him.

He snatched them from the air. "Come on."

I turned toward the ocean.

My blood went cold.

There was a storm on the horizon.

Only it was *so* much more than that.

I trembled. It wasn't like anything I'd ever seen. The sky above us was gray as sheet metal, but miles out on the water, there was nothing but black. Lightning flashed like daggers, stabbing the ocean below, and over the distance, thunder growled like an animal. The pitch-black clouds were swirling, their motion accented by flares of light, and with every second, they drew closer.

"Chloe!" Noah shouted.

Icy wind licked at me. Fear rooted me to the spot even as my mind screamed to run.

Noah's hands grabbed me, breaking the paralysis, and roughly, he pulled me around. My feet stumbled. Noah didn't stop. Hauling me with him, he rushed toward the car, his grip on my arm like iron.

Joseph hurried from the house, his arms full of papers and bottles. "The outer barriers are falling and the inner ones won't hold much longer. We have to–"

The wind picked up, stealing pages from his grip. He cried out in frustration but kept going, shuffling at high speed down the steps to the yard.

"Here, here, take this." From the mountain in his arms, he fumbled out a cork-sealed vial of black liquid and then shoved it into my hands. "You'll need to drink that. It'll start the splitting. You have to be careful, though. You'll pass out while that happens, so only take it when you're–"

Tires rumbled on the gravel track. Two vehicles pulled to a halt, both of them fully blocking the road. Still holding onto me, Noah swore.

I stared. This was like a nightmare.

Wyatt shoved open the door of the SUV before the thing even came to a stop. Cracks cut jagged paths through his skin, all of them glowing, and his eyes were like hell. From the brown sedan behind him, Harman scrambled out. Pain showed in every tense line of his face, but his eyes were eerily bright.

"Chloe! Eleanor!" The old man beamed at us, and the expression was so fractured with psychotic joy, it made me want to run. "So happy to find you girls here!"

Chief Reynolds and Aaron managed to climb out after him, but just barely. The chief stumbled and grabbed at the sedan to stop himself from falling. On the other side of the vehicle, Aaron just stood shaking, his gaze darting from Harman to me and back.

Wyatt stalked toward us.

"Hey!" Joseph snapped, stuffing the rest of his papers and bottles through the open door of Baylie's car. He marched at Wyatt. "You're not allowed here, greliaran! Move out of the way!"

"Get in," Noah ordered, pushing me toward the car. He headed around the vehicle to intercept his cousin, his skin transforming as he went.

I stayed where I was. Not looking away from Wyatt, I dropped the vial down with the papers in the back seat.

Joseph stopped directly in Wyatt's path.

The greliaran paused, eyeing the wizard incredulously. "And just what the hell are you supposed to be?"

"Move the car, Wyatt," Noah growled. "You see the sky back there? We don't have time for this."

Wyatt smirked. "Aw, little Noah's scared of lightning. I never knew."

He started toward Joseph.

"I'm warning you!" the wizard cried. "Get out of our way

now!"

Wyatt scoffed. He moved to shove the man aside.

Joseph flung out his arm. His hand slammed into Wyatt's chest.

The greliaran flew backward, speeding through the air. Bark shattered from the trunk of a tree when Wyatt crashed into it and I heard the branches shake hard with the impact. Limp as a rag, he tumbled to the ground.

"What the–" Chief Reynolds gasped. He fumbled for his gun.

Indignant, Clay and Owen scrambled from the other vehicle, their skin as changed as Wyatt's had been.

"Don't even think about it, you two!" Joseph yelled at them.

The SUV shuddered and then skidded sideways across the gravel road till it tumbled into the ditch.

Thunder growled. Wind gusted around me, tangling through my hair.

I didn't look back. I didn't need to. I could feel the storm getting closer. Stronger.

"Come with us, Chloe," Harman called. "It's not safe out here. Let us bring you home to your parents."

"Grandpa, please!" Ellie yelled. "Get out of here!"

He didn't even blink. "Everything's going to be fine, Eleanor. It's just a little storm."

Owen and Clay stared at their vehicle and then glanced to each other. Without a word, they spread out, heading for Joseph.

"This is your last chance!" Joseph shouted. He lifted his hand. "You grelia–"

Gunshots cut his words short. Joseph stumbled, clutching his chest in shock.

I gasped, looking from the wizard to Chief Reynolds. Holding the weapon with a white-knuckled grip, the chief turned the gun toward us.

"Get in the car!" he yelled, his voice ragged.

His nephew stared at him. "Chief, what are you–"

"Shut *up*, Aaron!" He adjusted his shaking hold on the gun. "This ends now! Girls, get in the goddamn car!"

Joseph straightened. Every crystal of his jewelry glowed. His whole body trembled with the effort of standing upright.

The wind blew harder. The wizard swayed with it.

Chief Reynolds turned the weapon toward him again. "You stay back or I'll–"

Clay and Owen ran at Joseph.

Noah moved to stop them.

The chief emptied the gun at him.

"No!" Baylie screamed.

I shoved away from the car, racing for Noah as he staggered and fell.

"Chief, what are you *doing*?" Aaron cried.

Owen and Clay raced past Noah without a glance.

Joseph raised a hand. Clay flew toward the trees.

And Owen slammed into the wizard. Snarling, he hurled the old man back through the air, and then charged after him like a dog with a toy.

I heard Joseph shout. Heard the sound cut off. I couldn't

look. The wind swirled, flinging dirt and grit up into my face while I crumpled to my knees next to Noah.

He was breathing in rapid gasps. With a furious grunt, he tried to shove up from the driveway.

"Stay there!" the chief yelled while he struggled to reload the gun.

"You bastard!" Baylie cried, putting herself in front of her stepbrother.

"Noah?" I grabbed his arm, but his skin was so hot, I couldn't hold on.

At my side, Ellie dropped to her knees as well. "Here," she said, pushing her bundled jacket into my hands. "Put pressure on whatever got through."

Noah made a choked noise, the sound almost as angry as it was pained. He shook his head. "I'm okay."

"You just stay down!" Chief Reynolds shouted.

"Come back over here, girls," Harman added. "Leave that boy there. He's not safe."

"Chief, *please*!" Aaron begged. "This isn't right!"

Noah grimaced. With a sharp breath, he pushed away from the ground and rose to his feet.

"Stay down!" the chief cried, taking aim again.

"Leave him alone!" Baylie shouted, keeping herself in front of Noah. Ellie scrambled up and hurried to join her.

"You girls get out of the way!" Chief Reynolds yelled. "I'm warning you! I don't want to have to–"

"Dammit, Uncle Barry! Drop the gun!"

The chief looked over.

Aaron had his weapon aimed at him.

"Boy, what the hell are you–"

"I'm stopping this! Those are kids. *Kids*! And you've damn near killed one! *I* nearly killed one! I *know* those girls! I just wanted to *help* people! I've done everything you and Doctor Brooks asked but now… now just put down the gun!"

"You can't–"

"*Put down the gun*!" Aaron shrieked.

The chief stared at him. Cautiously, his trembling grip eased from the weapon. Still watching his nephew, he lowered the gun to the roof of the sedan.

"Pass it over here," Aaron ordered.

The chief pushed the weapon toward him.

"Get in the car," Aaron continued. "You too, Doctor Brooks. We're leaving."

"Now, we can't do that," Harman countered. "Not without Chloe and Eleanor. The other girl too. The blonde one. She needs to come. It's not safe here."

"Damn you, Doctor Brooks! Get in the–"

Thunder rolled, drowning Aaron's words. The wind swirled around us, icy and tugging at me as if it wanted to pull me toward the sea.

I looked back in spite of myself.

The sky was growing darker. Winds drove the waves at the shore and sent them crashing against the bluffs. Black clouds churned and tumbled over each other as they raced toward land. Already they were nearly on top of us. No rain fell. Nothing left the storm but lightning. In blinding flashes, the bolts stabbed the sea like spears beating the water on their march toward land.

I shuddered. I wanted to run. To take off down the road – cars and guns and Harman Brooks be damned. But I could barely even breathe.

Ice sank into my skin. My body grew weak, as if the energy was being dragged from my muscles and bones straight into the roiling, impossible nightmare in the sky.

The roiling, impossible nightmare that *hated* me. There was no doubt. No question. I didn't know how I could feel emotion pouring off of that thing.

I just did. As clearly as if it was snarling at me, I did.

The storm wanted me dead.

Tears burned my eyes, driven by terror. My legs crumpled, their strength gone. Noah grabbed me as I fell. His skin was back to normal and his hands on my arms felt so solid. So real.

"Chloe, what the–"

Motion on the shore caught my gaze. Almost a dozen yards away, Owen was turning from Joseph. The greliaran was breathing hard, ecstasy slackening his face, and his whole body was shaking. The cracks in his skin spread wider when he straightened. Sparks flew from them like firecrackers lay inside.

And behind him, Joseph was dead. Bloody. He hadn't looked human before, but now…

My gorge rose. I couldn't do anything but stare.

Owen saw me watching him. Still panting, he pulled his lips back in a rabid sort of grin.

Noah swore. "He… Joseph had magic in him. Ocean magic like dehaians, and we… oh, hell…"

He pushed to his feet, his skin changing fast while he put himself between me and his cousin.

Owen's smile grew. He let out growl as he started forward.

And then he froze. His brow drew down, confusion on his inhuman face, and his body lurched. The cracks in his skin widened. A choked noise escaped him. Lifting his hands, he stared at them as the trembling increased and thick smoke began to pour out with the heat.

He looked up at us in horror.

Fire exploded from every crack in his skin.

Noah spun, trying to shelter me from the flames.

The heat never arrived. The wall of fire turned before it reached us, racing upward as if drawn away. Owen's body collapsed, blackened and charred, while in a column of light, the fire curved into the sky and flew into the storm.

Where it vanished.

I gasped. The draining feeling disappeared like a cord had been cut, setting me free. His skin swiftly becoming human again, Noah grabbed me. Clutching him, I scrambled for my feet on legs that quivered like jelly.

The storm seemed to slow. The churning of the clouds stilled.

But in the air, I could feel something change.

"Oh God," I whispered, my grip on Noah tightening.

"Car!" Noah shouted at Ellie and Baylie. "Now!"

They spun and raced for the car. Still holding me, Noah ran after them.

The wind started to pick up again, icy and scraping across my skin like it had razors inside. Overhead, the black clouds began to tumble and roll, racing for land faster than before.

"Keys!" Baylie shouted at Noah. "You help Chloe!"

Noah yanked the keys from his pocket and tossed them to her.

"Doctor Brooks!" Aaron yelled.

I looked back.

Harman was walking toward us. "Girls? Come along now. Those creatures are gone. It's all going to be fine."

The strange feeling in the air grew stronger. Wind blew in hard from the ocean, shoving us as we tried to reach the car.

Ellie caught herself on the door. "Grandpa, go back!"

"Get in!" Baylie shouted at her.

Harman continued closer, his expression consoling though he rocked with blasts of wind. "Now, I know it's been frightening here. But we still have lots of work to do together, so you have to come with–"

Lightning struck the trees behind him and the world exploded into light.

I stumbled backward and hit the ground. Everything tingled. Buzzed. The deafening boom rang in my ears while stars blinded my eyes. Blinking hard, I staggered up from the gravel, struggling to see.

On the far side of the yard, a hole had been cut in the forest wall. Smoke rose from the base of it, while blackened chunks of wood were scattered across the gravel – debris from what had once been a tree.

And Harman was on the ground.

"Grandpa!" Ellie cried.

She ran for him.

"Ellie!" Noah shouted.

Aaron shoved away from his car and chased after her.

By her grandfather's side, Ellie fell to her knees. "Grandpa, get up!" She shook his shoulders.

He didn't move.

"Grandpa!"

Aaron dropped down beside her. He felt for a pulse quickly, and then shook his head.

Ellie sobbed.

"Come on!" Aaron shouted over the howling wind. "We have to–"

Lightning struck a hundred yards offshore.

Aaron wasted no more words. Snagging Ellie, he hauled her upright. She stumbled, still looking toward her grandfather.

"Go!" Aaron yelled at us. "She'll be safe! Just go!"

He pulled her toward the sedan.

We scrambled to get into the car. Baylie shoved the key into the ignition while Noah and I tumbled into the back.

The engine growled. Up ahead, Chief Reynolds whipped his sedan through a tight turn and took off down the road.

Baylie yanked the gearshift into place and then floored the pedal, racing after him.

I spun in the seat. The forest swallowed the view of the house and the sea almost instantly. Leaves and pine needles lashed the car while wind howled through the trees and the ground beneath us shuddered. Lightning lit the clouds in unnatural shades of bloody red and stabbed the forest with such force that the car rocked from the blasts.

But the black storm seemed to be holding position. It wasn't spreading. It wasn't coming after us. The churning of the clouds had stopped and though the wind still shrieked around us, we seemed to be leaving the lightning behind.

My brow drew down. Why would it stop? It was true that I didn't feel weird anymore, and Joseph had said strange feelings were a sign the Beast knew where I was. But why would it stop searching?

Realization quivered through me, bringing horror on its heels. My gaze dropped to the road behind us. Joseph's house. If the lightning hit his machines…

I turned to the road ahead. Chief Reynolds and the others were several hundred yards in front of us, their sedan hurtling down the path as though propelled by nitrous. Her hands clutching the steering wheel, Baylie chased them at such a speed, we were barely keeping to the gravel.

But we weren't going fast enough. None of us were. Not if—

The world behind us went white. Stark light flooded the forest like a supernova.

And then the blast wave hit.

It was magic. It surged through the car, saturating everything, and I screamed as the change ripped through my body, disintegrating my clothes and making the air burn like acid on my skin. My legs melded into a tail instantly. My feet became a fin that smashed against the passenger seat and my lungs couldn't find any way to breathe.

I heard Baylie cry out as the car rocked forward, tipping sharply till the rear wheels left the ground.

The magic rushed upward and vanished as though sucked away.

With a thud, the car slammed back to all four wheels. Skidding hard on the gravel, it swerved and then kept going.

I gasped, fighting for oxygen. Everything hurt, from the air to the upholstery, and my tail was crammed amid the papers in the footwell at an angle that bent my fin painfully against the seat and door. My whole body felt electrified in a way I'd never experienced from the change and, for a moment, I lay paralyzed.

"Noah?" Baylie called. "Chloe?"

Choking on the pain, I rolled my head to the side, looking to Noah.

His skin was like fire and his eyes were squeezed shut. Smoke twisted up from the fissures on his arms and face. His body spasmed with every few heartbeats as though he was being shocked.

"Noah, breathe," Baylie urged, watching him in the rearview

mirror. "Fight. Don't let it win."

He snarled, his head shaking like her words hurt, and the sound wasn't like anything I'd ever heard from him. Wild. Inhuman. He gave a desperate gasp, his hands clenching the edge of the seat. His fingers ripped through the fabric while muscles torn by fissures stood out on his arms.

A new fear rushed through me. If he lost control… if what Joseph said was true…

I couldn't even move.

Baylie threw a glance to me. "Chloe, are you–" Her eyes went wide and she swore. "H-hang on, guys," she managed, turning back to the road. "Just… just hang on."

I didn't answer. I couldn't. My skin was burning. Black spots were swirling over my vision. My body wouldn't change and everything hurt so much and…

A tiny breath entered my lungs. I lurched up, drawing in more air while the black spots melted away. A heartbeat passed and then the burning on my skin lessened. My muscles still quivered with the strange feeling of the magic's passage, but the searing pain was fading.

My gaze went to Noah.

His eyes were still shut, but his shaking had mostly stopped. Breathing in short gasps, he shook his head and while I watched, the fissures in his skin started to close.

A pained growl escaped him as the last of the cracks faded. He opened his eyes. For a moment, they burned like red-hot coals, and then slowly they transformed back to deep green when they turned to me.

"Chloe?"

I stared at him. His brow flickered down at my fear, sorrow in his eyes.

"It's okay," he said quietly. "I promise."

His hand trembled when he reached out.

Hesitantly, I let him draw me closer.

"I'd never hurt you," he whispered as he pulled me into his arms. "Never."

Trembling, I leaned against him. His skin was warm and like the seat and the air, his touch hurt my skin.

But the pain was fading. And his arms were still so comforting.

"Can you change back?" he asked.

I swallowed hard, looking down at my tail curled into the paper-strewn footwell.

A moment crept by. The cream-colored scales slid from me, turning to iridescent dust that vanished even as it hit the floor. Only enough of them remained to cover my body like a swimsuit above my bare legs.

I shivered, still feeling strange. Noah's arms tightened on me, holding me close, and his hand ran down my hair, almost as if reassuring himself we were okay.

Baylie's car bounded onto the main road. Flying after Chief Reynolds' sedan, we sped down the country highway.

I turned carefully, wincing at the scrape of the seat fabric on my skin.

The black clouds hadn't followed us. Even the lightning was still. Miles back, the storm hung motionless in the sky over the space where the house had been.

"It's going to get stronger," Noah said, his voice rough.

I nodded. Like it had when Owen died, the storm had paused. But it wouldn't for long.

I trembled, watching the clouds while Baylie raced the car away from the coast.

It took two hours before any of us wanted to stop.

"Yeah, sure," Baylie said into the cell phone. "That one will do. I just need a minute to grab her some shoes."

She paused, and then hung up. "Aaron on Ellie's phone," she explained, glancing back at us. "We're going to pull over up here."

I nodded, but she'd already returned her attention to the busy interstate. Guiding the car onto an off-ramp, she followed the chief's sedan. The cars paused at a stoplight, and then traced a short path into the parking lot of a department store only a few hundred yards away.

"Back in a sec," Baylie said as she pushed the gearshift into park. She extended the keys to me. "Bag of clothes in the trunk."

I nodded. She opened the door and climbed out. Checking both directions quickly, she headed for the store.

Silence settled between me and Noah, and neither of us moved. We'd barely spoken since we left the forest. He'd just kept his arms around me and, every so often, I felt him shiver, like a residual charge was trembling through his skin.

It was the same for me. I couldn't stop shaking, any more than I could bring myself to leave the reassurance his arms provided. Something hadn't vanished with the rest of the magical blast wave and it frightened me. That hadn't been like any change I'd ever experienced and, even now, I didn't feel normal. From the way Noah looked, I wasn't sure he did either. True, my skin had stopped hurting a while ago, my legs hadn't shown any sign of scales, and I hadn't struggled to breathe since I'd been able to change back.

But I still felt weird.

I flinched when Aaron appeared by the window, a blanket in his hands. My brow furrowing, I pushed open the door.

He wouldn't look at me. "Ellie said you might've, well…" He jerked his chin nervously toward my body.

Discomfort hit me and I reached up, taking the blanket from him. Rising from the car, I wrapped the scratchy, gray fabric around myself quickly.

Aaron glanced to Noah when he got out as well. "Listen," he said to me. "I, um… I'm sorry. For what happened to you, I mean. I never… I thought you needed help. I didn't know everything."

I wasn't sure what to say. His gaze flicked up to me and then away again.

"And what Doctor Brooks did to that dehaian guy," he continued. "I'm sorry for that too. Your friend felt pain. He did and I should've done something to stop it. I just…" His mouth tightened and he shook his head. "I should have."

I paused. My gaze went to the brown sedan. By the door, Ellie stood, her eyes red from crying. In the driver's seat, the chief hadn't moved.

"Are you all okay?" I asked quietly.

He nodded. "We were ahead of the blast wave."

"I mean, are you okay from the ocean? Does it still hurt?"

Aaron hesitated. "I'm fine."

I watched him, almost certain he was lying. Tension showed around his eyes, like tiny lines where there should have been none, and now that I looked for it, I could see his hands trembling.

Reaching out, I took his wrist before he could pull away. Tingles coursed through me.

And they felt strange. Stronger. Electric. I struggled to rein the magic back again.

The tension on Aaron's face vanished into surprise. His breath caught and he blinked at me when I released him.

"Hey," Baylie called, jogging up to us. She spotted Aaron staring at me. "Everything alright?"

"Yeah," I managed.

She nodded slowly. "Okay… Well, here. Best I could do."

I took the bag. "Thanks."

Not looking at either of them, I headed around to the other side of the car, needing distance.

Something had happened to us. Maybe. Or maybe Noah

and I were just shaky from changing that fast and that's why things felt strange. Maybe it was nothing.

I tugged the tags from the sandals, not quite able to make myself believe that. The Beast had caused that explosion, and that explosion had contained God knew how much magic, of God knew what kinds.

Anything could have happened.

Attempting to push the thoughts away, I shoved my feet into the shoes. Opening the door, I bent to stuff the plastic bag into the small trash bin on the floor of the car.

My gaze caught on a glint of black.

Carefully, I reached down and drew the vial from beneath the edge of the driver's seat. Within the glass, the black liquid slipped back and forth, viscous and utterly opaque.

I heard footsteps come around the car.

"You alright?" Baylie asked. She paused. "What's that?"

I glanced over. "Joseph's potion to split what I am."

Her face went still.

I looked back at the vial. I knew I should take it. Now. This moment, before the Beast became any stronger. Before it could hunt me down, even this far inland.

But I didn't want to lose my dehaian side. I didn't want to lose Noah. Zeke. The ocean. Everything.

I didn't want to risk that this was the end.

"So," Baylie asked, her voice choked. "What are you going to do?"

EPILOGUE

WYATT

I opened my eyes.

Kindling and shredded branches lay across me like a tree had exploded into matchsticks nearby. Smoke carried on the air, billowing from the burning pile of wood and rubble that had been a house.

And overhead, the blackest storm I'd ever seen churned like a nightmare straight from hell.

I stared up at it. There was no rain. Barely any wind either. Everything was still but the clouds, which rolled over and into each other with a speed that should have been impossible.

And that wasn't all.

I shuddered. I felt strange. Like my skin had changed while I'd been unconscious – something that should have been impossible. And electrified too, as if I'd stuck my finger into a socket, or maybe even my entire arm.

The wind picked up. A whisper carried on it, the words harsh and cold and sounding sort of like the bits of gibberish my grandfather had claimed were fish language.

I pushed to my feet and looked around fast, trying to find the source.

The whisper cut off.

My brow furrowed. Nothing much lay nearby but shattered trees and smoking debris. A short distance from me, Clay was struggling to rise, his body half-buried beneath kindling much like mine had been. On the far side of the gravel yard, the maroon-robed freak was crumpled and, from the bloodied mess of his body, very clearly dead. A few yards from him was a charred corpse, only a few unburned scraps of fabric hanging from it.

I recognized Owen's clothes. I glanced around again, wondering what'd been able to do that to him.

The whispering resumed, darker and colder than before. I froze, incredulity hitting me at the same time as understanding.

My gaze tracked upward.

The storm. The whisper was coming from the storm.

My heart started to pound harder. It wasn't really in my ears, though. It was in my head. I could feel it. Like a presence, watching me. Studying me. Speaking to me. The words were still gibberish, but somehow, that didn't matter anymore.

A chuckle left me. My lips pulled back, curling into a smile.

I knew what it wanted me to do.

Chloe, Zeke, and Noah's story will continue.

Join my new release mailing list at skyemalone.com to keep up with my newest books!

Loved the book?

Awesome! Would you like to leave a review? Visit Goodreads or any other book-related site and tell people about it!

Other titles

The Touch Me series

The Awakened Fate series

The Children and the Blood trilogy (published under the name Megan Joel Peterson)

About the author

Skye Malone is a fantasy and paranormal romance author, which means she spends most of her time not-quite-convinced that the magical things she imagines couldn't actually exist.

A Midwestern girl who migrated to the Pacific Northwest, she hopes to someday travel the world – though in the meantime she'll take any story that whisks her off to a place where the fantastic lives inside the everyday. She loves strong and passionate characters, complex villains, and satisfying endings that stay with you long after the book is done. An inveterate writer, she can't go a day without getting her hands on a keyboard, and can usually be found typing away while she listens to all the adventures unfolding in her head.

Connect with me

Website: www.skyemalone.com

Twitter: twitter.com/Skye_Malone

Facebook: facebook.com/authorskyemalone